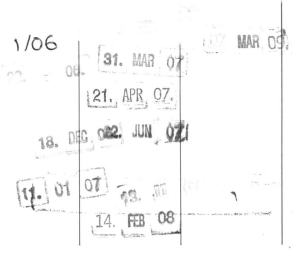
Books should be returned or renewed by the
last date stamped above.

Glasby, John

LP

The Savage City

THE SAVAGE CITY

She was the kind of woman a man noticed, mostly because of her eyes. Deep and dark, they had held a warmth which could easily kindle into a fire. Now they were staring sightlessly from the sidewalk. A killing without a motive, the first of a string of murders that led Johnny Merak, private investigator, from the teeming underworld of Chicago and Los Angeles to the edge of the New Mexico desert, trailing a killer who left no clues. But Merak knew the underworld, its methods and its hiding places.

JOHN GLASBY

THE SAVAGE CITY

Complete and Unabridged

LINFORD
Leicester

Originally published in paperback in 1960

First Linford Edition
published 2005

British Library CIP Data

Glasby, John S. (John Stephen)
  The savage city.—Large print ed.—
  Linford mystery library
  1. Murder—Investigation—United States—
  Fiction 2. Serial murders—United States—
  Fiction 3. Detective and mystery stories
  4. Large type books
  I. Title
  823.9′14 [F]

  ISBN 1–84395–751–5

Published by
F. A. Thorpe (Publishing)
Anstey, Leicestershire

Set by Words & Graphics Ltd.
Anstey, Leicestershire
Printed and bound in Great Britain by
T. J. International Ltd., Padstow, Cornwall

This book is printed on acid-free paper

1

The Red Edge of Terror

The downtown quarter of Los Angeles was no fancy place on that particular November evening. Overhead, there was a thin slice of moon showing above the wavering fog and somewhere in the distance, coming closer, a siren was wailing like a lost soul in some private hell. Beside me, Dawn Grahame handled the big Mercury easily, slipping in and out of the heavy light-night traffic, heading into the industrial suburbs. Whatever was storming through her mind at that moment, didn't show on her face.

She rounded a long curve. The brilliant lights appeared one after the other through the fog, tinged with green haloes. Through the window, I caught a glimpse of a floodlit panorama of neon-embroidered bars, interspersed with the occasional filling station, a blur of figures on the sidewalks, hazed by the swirling fog.

My watch said nine-thirty. Less than twenty minutes since that call from Harry Grenville. It hadn't told me much, but he was that kind of a guy, saying little over the phone as if he believed that everyone was tapping it. As a Federal man he had come up against this too often in the past to forget it altogether.

We slid between a couple of parked trucks, into a narrow street. There was another long block ahead of us, filled with darkness, a filling station at the far end where the street opened out into another dingy thoroughfare, but everything was locked up for the night, in darkness.

I wondered why Grenville had sounded so urgent over the phone. A matter of life and death, he had said. It didn't make sense, but then there were so many things in Los Angeles, or any other big American city for that matter, which didn't add up.

'There,' said Dawn suddenly. She slowed the car, pointed through the windscreen.

I stared ahead. A single light shone

halfway along the drab street. Nearby, a couple of tattered 'For Rent' signs swung limply in the fog from one of the buildings. The doors and windows hung with peeling strips of paint. In the street itself, three cars were clustered near the edge of the sidewalk where the solitary lamp threw a circle of diffuse yellow light through the murk.

Dawn stopped the car, switched off the ignition and got out. I followed. A new set of thoughts popped up inside my brain and began nibbling at the edges. I figured there had been an accident of some kind here, but why had Grenville sounded so worried and more to the point, what had it got to do with me? I started looking for Grenville and spotted him inside a cluster of cops. They turned as I walked up to them with Dawn on my heels. One of the cops threw me a funny glance. He looked cynical and politely surprised. I could guess that he was puzzled.

Maybe he even knew who I was and was trying to figure out in his well-organised mind what a guy like Johnny Merak was doing on a job like this.

'Glad you got here, Johnny.' A brief smile from Grenville, a tight-lipped smile that scarcely twisted the corners of his mouth. 'Something I thought you ought to be in on from the beginning. You may be one of the few men who can help us.'

I shrugged my shoulders. I still didn't see where I fitted in, but it figured that, with a guy like Grenville, who knew all the angles, there had to be a reason for it somewhere and I was content to bide my time.

'Something wrong, Harry?'

'Plenty. It isn't nice, so if — ' He threw a quick, appraising look at Dawn.

She caught the implication behind it immediately, nodded and stepped back a couple of paces. Then Harry Grenville moved aside and I saw, for the first time, what lay on the sidewalk behind him.

She lay half across the sidewalk with her head lying in the gutter. It needed only one look to see that she was dead, very dead. I went forward, knelt down on one knee. She was the kind of woman a man would have noticed, would have glanced at for a second time, mostly

4

because of her eyes. The rest of her face wasn't particularly beautiful, too sharply-angled and aloof, but her eyes had once been dark and deep and full of life and vitality. Eyes which could easily have become kindled into a warmth which might have turned into a fire.

Now they were empty and glazed and fixed, staring at something high over my head, at the moon, or at the fog — or just at death, it was hard to tell. A tall woman with slender legs and slender arms, a simple red-and-white checked dress beneath the belted coat. There was blood on the front of the dress and it didn't need an expert to tell that there were at least half a dozen .38 slugs in her body, fired from pretty close range.

I got to my feet. My lighter flamed in my hand as I lit the cigarette.

Then I turned to Grenville. There must have been a question on my face for he said quickly. 'So a dame gets herself bumped off and you still can't figure the angle for me bringing you into it.'

'That's right.'

'I'm merely playing a hunch this time,

Johnny. Sure, I know that thousands of dames and guys get themselves killed in Los Angeles every year and we never hear about most of them. But this one is different.'

'How different?'

'That's what I want to know. It looks like a gang killing to me, but there's no motive so far.'

'You know who she is?'

'We've checked. Her name was Lomer, Caroline Lomer. Lived in some place a couple of blocks from here. It would have been easy for anybody who wanted to murder her to get the lowdown on her movements.'

'Sounds like a thousand other dames,' I said. 'I don't see the connection.'

'You might as well know everything, Johnny.' The other sounded tired; as if he had run up against something which was a little beyond him. 'We had a call from this woman three days ago. At least, the local precinct did. She was scared. Somebody — she didn't say who — wanted to kill her. She asked for protection.'

'If she got it, it doesn't look as if it did her much good,' I remarked. I saw the tall, burly cop move forward as if to say something, then he obviously thought better of it and kept quiet.

'We checked on her from the start.' Grenville even sounded slightly amused. 'For all we knew, she might have been a screwball. There are plenty of them around here with a persecution mania. Nobody knew much about her. It didn't figure at all. There was no doubt that she was scared of something. But we found nothing to tie her in with any of the gangs.'

'I see,' I said. I didn't, for at the moment, there were too many loose ends lying around waiting to be tied up. Too many unknowns, one body too many, and six slugs which couldn't be explained.

'We want you in on this case because of — well, your background. You know the Underworld, Johnny. You know how it operates, you know its methods, probably better than any other man outside of the Organisation. I'm convinced myself, this isn't just another slaying like the thousands of others we come across. There's something here that doesn't fit, and by God, I intend to find out what it is.'

'O.K. Harry,' I said. 'Count me in. But if it doesn't turn out that way, don't blame me.'

'I won't, Johnny.' He was looking straight at me, trying to see my face in the light of the street lamp. 'How do you figure on beginning?'

'At the moment, I've no idea,' I said honestly. The whole affair was still a little crazy, mixed-up. A woman died with six slugs in her body in a backstreet of downtown Los Angeles — so what? It happened before, a countless number of times, and it would happen again. But if a man like Harry Grenville believed that there was something more than an ordinary slaying here, then who was I to doubt him. Far too often, in the past, he had been right with these hunches of his. It wouldn't hurt, anyway, if I strung along with him, at least for the time being.

Besides, I knew exactly how the Underworld worked, how it was nurtured. It was a vast, spider-like thing squatting in the heart of the city, its tentacles spread out throughout the whole of the surrounding territory. There wasn't a single spot where a man would be able to hide if the Organisation wanted him dead. This tremendous octopus was fed and swollen by the fears and intimidation of little men. The fast cars without lights that struck without warning leaving a huddled body in the middle of the street. The pathetic corpses which were brought to the surface from the river. The broken, spiritless creatures who existed in the twilight world of the backstreets, kidneys ruptured by carefully wielded hoses which left no mark outside. Or the bullets fired from close range on the sidewalk with no witnesses but the slayer and the victim.

This could be the same. There was nothing to prove it either way at the moment, apart from Grenville's hunch. I threw another look down at the body on the sidewalk. A pretty figure and a face which had once been pleasant and full of life; but not now. Now, something had been wiped out of it and the face had that look of surprise and shock and fear which told only too plainly that in the second before she had died, she had known who her killer was, had known that death was there, inevitable and frightening.

I walked back into the ring of cops. I could feel their eyes on me, wondering — who the hell is this guy Johnny Merak, ex-crook turned private detective? But if there was any suspicion in their eyes it didn't register. I stood looking at Dawn for a long moment and I knew that the same thought was in her mind as was in mine. It had all started again. The lonely fight against the Underworld, the big boys, the ruthless men who posed on the outside as decent, law-abiding citizens of the community. But on the inside, away from the publicity, they dabbled in the dirtiest work there was. Blackmail and murder came high on their list. Graft and corruption a close second. Only they didn't do this dirty work themselves. They had the hired gunmen, the grafters, the fixer to do it for them. They merely gave the orders and sat back in the middle of the web and watched the drama played out to their liking.

If the order went out that someone had to die; then they died. Very few were as lucky as I had been, to get out of that web of vice and treachery and death and still remain alive and in one piece. Most who tried it, ended up as drunks and physical wrecks after the hoodlums had worked them over for laughs.

No — it was easy to see how Caroline Lomer could have died. But proving it would be a difficult matter — and discovering who did it, whose hand was at the back of the killing, more difficult still.

'You're going to try to find out who did it, Johnny.' Dawn's voice was soft and husky. It wasn't a question.

I nodded. 'I said I was through with all of the dirty stuff a long time ago. I promised myself then, that if there was ever anything I could do to get back at them, to break them, I'd do it. Maybe this is another chance.'

'You might not be so lucky this time, Johnny.' Still no question of trying to get me to back out.

'I know, Dawn. But now that I feel clean again, I want to keep it that way. I wouldn't if I backed out of this deal.'

'All right, Johnny. I'd rather see you die trying than quit. But there's nowhere for you to start.'

I climbed back into the Mercury while she slipped in behind the wheel. The light still shone on the crumpled body lying near the gutter and I couldn't get the look in that kid's eyes out of my mind. The little thoughts were having another scamper around my brain as I sat there, while Dawn slipped in behind the wheel. The more I thought about it, the more odd this whole set-up seemed. There wasn't such a thing as a motive-less murder; and if the Underworld did have any part in it, even if they had only sanctioned the murder, as seemed possible, the motive was there somewhere if it could only be found. Maybe it was buried under a mountain of useless facts. Maybe it was there, staring me in the face, in the middle of that cluster of cops, if I could only see it.

Harry Grenville came over and peered into the window. His granite-like face was in shadow.

'What do you think, Johnny?'

'It could be what you think,' I said after a pause. 'Whoever killed her picked a quiet spot for the murder. That means they did know her movements and I'm pretty sure she knew who shot her. If this was a mob killing, it oughtn't to be too difficult to find out.'

'That going to be your first move, Johnny?' Quiet concern in the other's voice, but I guessed it was more than that. He wanted to know my movements just to keep a check on me, to know where I'd be if he wanted to get in touch with me fast.

'There's nothing I can do tonight,' I said. 'Whoever did it will be miles away by now. You could question the folk in the neighbourhood, but I reckon you'll get very little out of them. Once they get it into their heads that this is a mob slaying, they'll close up like clams. You won't be able to prise any information out of them with a whip.'

'I guess you're right. I'll have the body taken to the mortuary once the rest of the boys are finished. Where can I get in touch with you tomorrow if anything turns up?'

'Difficult to say. If I have to go after information, I could be anywhere. Maybe I'd better call you. Noon.'

'O.K. Johnny. But watch yourself. I've a hunch you're right in this hunch.'

'Then play it smart. And if you need any help, I'll do everything I can. You know that.'

'Sure, Harry. I'll be seeing you.'

He stepped back onto the sidewalk as the car moved away from the kerb. Dawn drove silently through the flowing traffic. The fog was lowering and I couldn't see the moon. It was difficult to see the lights along the fronts of the bars and the all-night cinemas.

Caroline Lomer. I tried to make guesses at what could have happened. Haunted by fear, scared stiff of something she couldn't fight, something she couldn't live with any longer, she had gone to the police, asking for protection, demanding security, searching for a way out of her fear. Thinking about her, I realised that we had been possibly two of a kind. Only

I had been a little more fortunate. I had escaped from the rackets with a whole skin. She had died, trying.

Don't kid yourself either way, Merak. These men are killers. They know you from the old days. They also know that if anybody can smash them, you can. Do you think they're going to give you the chance again? It's a good life you've got now. You've earned it so why throw it away? If this is an Underworld killing, if the Organisation is at the back of it, you don't stand the ghost of a chance going through with it.

I pushed the thoughts away into the back of my mind and glanced through the windscreen. We were nearly there. Another couple of blocks to the Office. Dawn began to edge the Mercury in towards the kerb when the other car, without headlights, came screeching around the corner some thirty yards away, leaping towards us out of the fog. For the first time in my life, I was thankful for the days spent in the web of the Underworld. The mere fact that the car carried no headlights was enough to start a chain reaction inside my brain which transferred itself automatically to my body.

There was an outlet road some ten yards ahead on the same side. I thrust Dawn to one side, felt her fall away from me against the door with a little scream of surprise blended with realisation on her lips. Her fingers slipped instinctively from the wheel and I grabbed it in the split second before the oncoming car hit the middle of the road, steadied, then headed straight for us.

I knocked Dawn's foot off the pedal, swung the wheel sharply, violently. We were moving much too fast to take that corner safely, but it was our only chance if we wanted to stay alive. Tyres screeched thinly in protest. The other car, a big black Cadillac was almost on top of us. He must have guessed at my intention for he was half turning as I hit the corner and slewed into it in a side-swipe. The headlights of the Mercury glared brilliantly, brightening the curve to the side street. It was a narrow, almost right-angled curve. The car began to swerve to one side, skidding violently.

Dawn screamed again, pulled herself against me as I thrust her head down, beneath the edge of the windscreen with my right elbow, twisted in the seat. We hit the centre of the road and the car lurched as we made the turn. The wheels hit the far kerb and for one wild instant, the car tilted and threatened to go over onto its side.

Then, miraculously, it straightened. My hands were hard on the wheel as I fought desperately for control. From behind me, I heard a harsh stuttering and the side mirror vanished in a splintering of glass. Something smacked against the side of the windscreen and everything blurred as the glass splintered and cracked under the shattering impact of the slug.

The car bounced again, less violently this time and I eased my foot down on the brake. We went across the sidewalk, came to rest against the wall of the nearby building. We were hurled into the wheel and dash, but not too badly.

Fighting for breath, I pushed myself upright, threw a swift glance at Dawn.

Slowly, she lifted herself and stared up at me.

'Are you all right?'

'I think so, Johnny, that was a mad thing to do.'

'I know. But it was the only thing to do. Those hoodlums meant business. When they figured they couldn't ram us, they took a couple of shots at us. That slug must have missed us by a couple of inches, no more.'

'But why, Johnny?'

'Isn't it obvious. It answers a lot of questions that have been worrying me. Now at least, I know where I stand. I know what I've got to face.'

'They know that you're in on this particular deal, and they're afraid. That's it, isn't it?'

'I guess so. It all adds up. Only I didn't figure they'd try anything so soon. There must have been somebody there who saw me and figured why I was there. They'd know Grenville, what kind of a guy he is.'

There was silence for a minute. I knew what she was thinking. I wondered what she would say next, and when she said it,

I felt no surprise.

'Whichever way you want to play it, Johnny, it's all right by me.' The warmth was back in her voice and it did funny little things to me even with the aches and bruises in my shook up body. I grinned back at her. Suddenly, for no reason at all, I felt on top of the world again. Some of the old exhilaration was back again, the challenge. I forgot for a long moment, about what might lie ahead for us, a lot of trouble and a lot of regrets.

I opened the door. It seemed to take all of the strength I had to push it open and clamber out. There wasn't a sound from the other street. The hoodlums could have stopped their car, switched off the engine, and be creeping up on me with silenced revolvers at that very moment. Only some half-remembered instinct told me that they hadn't; that they were no longer around. They wouldn't bother to hang around to see if they had finished us off. If they hadn't, there would be plenty of other times to try. I'd be around until then. That was one thing they could be sure of.

Dawn got out and stood swaying a little. I walked round and took a quick look at the car. It had been badly scratched on the one side, but it was still in a fit shape to take us to where we wanted to go.

'Let's get back to the Office, Dawn,' I said. I looked at my watch.

'I'm kind of shaky.'

'I'll drive.'

'Do you think they'll come back tonight, Johnny?'

'Not tonight. That's their pitch finished for the time being. They'll figure on something else for the next try, something a little more sophisticated. That was a mug's game to try with anybody who knows their methods. They'll think up something real good for the next time.'

A new set of aches popped out of my limbs as I eased myself behind the wheel, switched on the ignition again. The car was warm-hearted, responded almost instantly. Gently, I eased her away from the kerb, straightened her up. Everything seemed to be in good working order.

Back in the Office, with the curtains

drawn across the windows, Dawn fixed a couple of drinks. She was shaken, but doing her best not to show it.

Maybe, I thought watching her, she's already regretting telling me to go through with this deal. But she'll never show it, never let me know it.

I drained my glass and lit a cigarette. Inwardly, I wondered whether to ring Grenville and tell him what had happened. It would prove his theory to the hilt and he might like to know it; but on the other hand, he might try to make a move, to push things, and that could be fatal, especially as far as Johnny Merak, and possibly Dawn Grahame, were concerned.

No, it would be better to play this thing alone, at least for the time being. It still didn't make a lot of sense. Sure I knew now that the big boys were in on the deal, but why pick on some dame like Caroline Lomer unless she knew a lot more than was good for her and intended to spill it all to the cops. That would have been a good enough reason for them to want her out of the way. But even that idea didn't quite figure right.

Damn it all, I thought fiercely, there had to be an answer to this somewhere. Do something, Merak. Don't just sit there thinking about these things. Somewhere out there in the teeming city, was somebody who knew the right answers to the questions. Find him and get them out of him.

I stubbed out the cigarette. I knew that Dawn was watching me in silence, wondering what was going on in my brain. The big trouble was that it was hard to forget that I had once been in the rackets myself. Then, if I needed any information, I merely had to beat it out of the guy concerned. A quick ride, the once-over and you had everything you wanted to know. Now — well, it wasn't quite as simple. True, Harry Grenville often turned a blind eye to what went on, provided it stopped short of actual murder. But you usually had to go about things in a more discreet way, although the rules were still unchanged for the other side.

I remembered the bullets that had

smashed through the windscreen of the car close to my head only a half hour before, and wondered what fresh plan was being built up against me, and by whom. The Underworld was a vast thing with a lot of men pulling the strings.

Maybe even now, the killer was squatting in a black web of vice and murder, waiting to strike again, planning ahead, preparing to commit a further murder to wipe out any lead I might find. At the moment, I was completely lost, stumbling around in the dark.

Dawn went out to fix some food and I sat in silence, trying to think things out. Trouble had a habit of following me around and I didn't want any of it to brush off onto her if I could possibly help it. By now, the word seemed to have got around that Johnny Merak was nosing into everyone else's business, private and otherwise, and I doubted whether many people would be really sorry if I departed the world quite suddenly with a slug in my brain. Nobody that is, except for Dawn Grahame, and possibly Harry Grenville. Maybe it was because of this that I was intent of keeping myself alive and seeing things through to the bitter end.

The phone shrilled, breaking in on my thoughts. I picked it up after a moment's pause. It could have been the guy who had tried to kill me, ringing up to find out if I was still alive.

'Johnny Merak?' The voice was harsh and metallic.

'That's right,' I said.

A pause, and then: 'I think you and I ought to have a little talk, Merak. It's important.'

'I don't usually make a point of talking to anybody I don't know and who doesn't give his name.'

'It concerns the murder of Caroline Lomer,' went on the voice in my ear.

'Go on.'

'I understand that you are on the case. I also happen to know that somebody tried to fix it for you permanently tonight.'

'You seem to know quite a lot.'

'I make it my business to know a lot of things, Mister Merak.' There was a sardonic chuckle in the voice as if the other was secretly amused. 'Sometimes, I find it pays dividends.'

'It could also be dangerous.'

'Perhaps. But like you, I'm an expert in taking chances.' For a moment, there was only the humming of the wires, then the other went on. 'I still think you ought to see me, Mister Merak. Shall we say tomorrow morning, nine o'clock at the Golden Horseshoe?'

'And I suppose I'd walk into a couple of your hired gunmen and get a bellyful of slugs for my trouble,' I said sarcastically.

'I guess that's a chance you'll have to take.' The phone clicked, the line went dead.

I replaced the receiver in its cradle and sat back in my chair. Dawn came into the room, looked at me curiously.

'I thought I heard the phone,' she said quietly.

'You did,' I nodded. 'Some guy who wouldn't give his name. Wanted to meet me at nine tomorrow. Said he had information for me about tonight's murder.'

'Are you going?'

'I'm not sure. It sounds too much like a trap to me. After they failed tonight, it's just the sort of thing they might try. On the other hand, it may be genuine and he didn't want to give his name for fear of retaliation.'

'It sounds like a trap.'

'I know. That's what I'm afraid of. At the moment, I'm trying to figure some way of getting around it if it is. I suppose I could call Grenville and tell him what's happened. He might be able to figure a way of watching the place in case of trouble and I could take this — ' I picked up the Luger, checked its buttered smoothness, then replaced it in my pocket, ' — only I'm afraid that if I did that, this guy, whoever he is, might smell a rat and he wouldn't turn up. That could destroy the only lead I've got.'

The multitude of thoughts had a fine chance to run around my brain as I ate the meal Dawn had prepared; but deep down inside, I knew that the outcome was certain. That I would go down there alone and see this man, take the chance on it

26

being a trap. Somehow, I thought fiercely, this game was becoming a little more complex and dangerous than I had figured at the beginning.

2

Tony Vitelli

There was something uncertain about the city the following morning. I sensed it as I eased the car away from the kerb and headed out in the main stream of traffic. The mist still hung around in patches, shreds of grey stuff which occasionally hid the fronts of the stores and the people going about their everyday activities. I worked my way downtown, keeping my eyes peeled for anything which might give me a lead on what I was heading into. There wasn't much. I needed another drink but it was still too early for any but the more flashy bars to be open in this district, although the Golden Horseshoe would have stayed open until around four in the morning, and would be open again once I reached it.

I stopped the car at the end of the dingy street, sat behind the wheel smoking. It still wanted ten minutes to nine o'clock, but on a blind date like this, I needed time in which to watch the joint, I needed to know the entrances and exits, whether the place was being watched by anyone apart from myself; and if so, by whom. More than once in the past, this caution had paid handsome dividends. Some guys had died quickly, if not cleanly, because they'd overlooked the most elementary details and had walked in to death with their eyes shut.

I finished the cigarette and decided that there was nobody watching the front entrance to the Golden Horseshoe. That didn't mean it was clear, but it certainly began to look as if my unknown informant was on the level.

Five minute's wait before I stubbed out my cigarette, checked the Luger in my pocket, then got out of the car. Far enough from the entrance to make things difficult for anybody trying to shadow me in, but close enough if I had to make a run for it. Five minutes more cut out of half an hour. I laughed at myself, nervous and impatient, like a kid fresh out of high school waiting for his first date.

I crossed the street quickly, melted into the shadows on the other side, then cut down a narrow alley which led to the back of the line of buildings. Maybe I'd tagged this guy wrong. Maybe he was a right guy trying to help me along. But there weren't many who'd do that for Johnny Merak, who had deliberately spat in the faces of the big men of the Underworld and turned his back on them. Anybody helping me was virtually signing his own death warrant if the big boys found out. That was one of the reasons it was so difficult to get information now, why I had to follow every possible lead, taking the risk of it being a trap.

The rear of the buildings, like the front, was no fancy place. I made it through a dark, garbage-strewn alley which angled between a couple of the buildings, spotted the one I wanted, and eased my way quietly along it. There was a high wall at the end of it and I pulled myself over it. My feet didn't make a sound when they hit the concrete on the other side and I was away into the shadows before any bright boys inside, who may have been on the look out for me, thought of looking in my direction. After that, it was comparatively easy.

I pushed open the back door and stepped into a narrow corridor. There was the smell of stale beer and tobacco smoke in my nostrils. There was another door at the end of the passage. I felt the comforting hardness of the Luger in my pocket before pushing my way through the door. The bar was half empty. Some guy was seated at the piano in one corner, thumping out a tuneless rhythm on the keys, head dropping forward as if he was drunk or half asleep.

The barman gave me a funny look, sizing me up with his eyes. I could almost hear his brain ticking over. Maybe he recognised me, maybe not. But there wasn't any doubt he was in the pay of the big boys, he would report anything unusual, no matter how trivial it might seem.

'Looking for somebody, friend?' asked the barman too casually, 'or are you just down for the drink?'

'Both,' I said. I knew better than to enlarge on that. Either he would shut up like a clam or slip off at the first opportunity and phone someone in the Organisation that there was a guy there asking too many questions about the wrong things.

Somebody crushed into the seat beside me. I knew better than to turn round right away. The barman moved away and the voice beside me said:

'Hello, Johnny. Glad you decided to come.'

I looked round, forced evenness into my voice. 'Tony Vitelli. I thought I recognised the voice over the phone, but I couldn't be sure.'

He sat huddled up on the bar stool, staring straight ahead of him into the mirror at the back of the bar. A short, suave guy, well-dressed, but not flashily so like most of the others. From the outside, you'd have taken him for a regular business guy, the kind you meet in the middle of Los Angeles any day around five, going back to a respectable surburban home, a wife and a couple of kids.

That was on the outside. On the inside, he was a professional killer who had learned his business the hard way in Detroit and Chicago. I knew his past record; arrested twice on suspicion of murder, more times than I could count for illegal possession of dope. But none of the charges had ever been made to stick and all of that was pretty old stuff from a few years back.

'Tell me about yourself, Tony,' I said easily.

'You in on this case about Caroline Lomer,' he said. 'This Federal guy Grenville is pretty sure that it's a mob slaying and he's put you onto the scent to try to smoke out the killer. Right?'

'Could be. Don't tell me that the Organisation has given you the job of seeing that I'm kept out of the case?'

The drinks came and I sipped mine slowly. Vitelli threw his over in a single gulp, turning the empty glass over slowly in his hands. If he had felt the insult, he gave no sign, his features never changed, his eyes never wavered.

'We used to work for the same people,

Johnny,' he said thickly. 'But that was a long time ago. Things have changed since then. You made the right move at the right time, when Clancy Snow and Dutch McKnight were rubbed out. It isn't so easy for guys like me. I want to make a little more than salary and cakes, but they've got so much pinned on me they'll never let me off the hook. If they don't get me themselves, they'll see to it that the cops get a full dossier on my past and there's enough in that to burn me ten times over.'

'So where do you come in now. What was all that talk over the phone. If you've got any information you'd better let me have it before any of your friends find you.'

Of course, I knew what was coming. Get mixed up in a dirty deal and you meet dirty people.

'Sure, Johnny. But what's in it for me? Can you put in a word with this Federal friend of yours, try to get me off the hook if I give you this information?'

'So that's it.' I looked him straight in the eye. A dangerous man in spite of his outward appearance of respectability. A changed guy? A solid, dependable citizen ready to take his place in society? Somehow, I didn't think so. There was more to this than showed on the surface, but I was damned if I could see it. I fingered the gun in my pocket, saw his glance stray downward, a little muscle twitching in his cheek.

'You'll do it for me, Johnny. After all, we're old friends.'

Like hell we are, I thought savagely, but I didn't say it out aloud. Tony Vitelli was my only lead and whether I liked him or not, I was stuck with him if I wanted to get anywhere with this case.

'I can't do that, Tony, and you know it,' I said steadily, watching him narrowly. I saw the sudden stiffening of his face, the sharp movement of his fingers on the polished top of the bar. He seemed to be taking a tight hold of himself, trying to make a decision. In the past, as one of the right hand men of the big bosses, he had been in the position of giving orders and knowing that they would be carried out to the letter, that if he said someone had to die, then the guy was knocked off and few questions were asked, even by the cops.

'O.K. Johnny. I guess I made a wrong pitch asking you to come along.' He slid off the bar stool, moved away.

I didn't know what was in his mind. All I did know was that here was the only lead I had and I was determined not to let it slip through my fingers. If I hadn't been nervous about the men I was dealing with, I may not have been so quick to be rough with a man like Tony. There were a lot of ideas churning away inside me — the memory of a woman lying slain on a lonely sidewalk, the big men hiding in a net of treachery and vice, fear, tension and disgust.

Reaching over, I took Tony's left hand in my right, pressing down hard on his thumb, twisting him round until his wrist was jammed hard against his shoulder blades. He hadn't made a sound. None too gently, I propelled him from the bar, towards the corridor leading out to the back. I knew it was unoccupied unless they had shifted some of their hirelings into it during the few minutes I had been talking in the bar.

'This isn't going to get you anything, Merak,' he mumbled as I pushed him through the swing door, into the passage.

'Maybe not,' I said, shoving his head forward. The barman watched us out of the corner of his eye, but he wanted no part in this quarrel. He knew better than to get mixed up in anything like this which was not his concern. He might get in touch with some of the big men, but not right away and by the time he contacted them, I hoped to be a long way away.

By the time we reached the end of the corridor, he was making little hurt noises in his throat. I located the gun in his hip pocket and slipped it into my own. Obviously he had come prepared to bargain the hard way if things had gone against him. It still didn't look like a trap, but I couldn't be sure and I didn't want to wait around long to find out. That was why I had to have the answers to my questions — and fast.

'Going to talk, Tony?'

He tried to nod his head against my

arm. Watchfully, I let him free.

'That's better. Just what is your connection with this murder? It wouldn't have been you who pulled it off, would it, Tony?' It was a definite possibility. It bore the same kind of handmark as some of his past handiwork, but somehow, I doubted it. He gave the orders instead of carrying them out.

'I work for Callen, you know that, Johnny,' he said thickly. 'You don't have to be so tough.'

'Then don't be tricky, Tony. You make me jumpy.' Harry Callen ran a big advertising agency in uptown Los Angeles and had a finger in more than a dozen motels strung out along the major highways in the state. All in the open and perfectly legitimate. Behind the scenes, he headed a gang of thugs who managed the protection racket and worked several big syndicates, ready to get evidence for blackmail, eager to rustle off anybody who made trouble.

I knew what happened to guys who tried to set themselves up against Harry Callen. They usually disappeared off the face of the earth with no trouble and no fuss, only turning up some time later when they were dredged out of the river. I didn't want to be one of those guys, but if I was to get anywhere, this was one of the risks I had to take.

'Talk, Tony,' I said swiftly. 'I don't want to have to rough you up any more than I have to, but believe me, I will if you don't tell me what I want to know.'

He rubbed his throat, a crafty gleam in his eyes. I didn't trust him as far as I could throw him with one hand tied behind my back, but I wanted to know what he had been so anxious to sell.

'I know who killed Caroline Lomer.'

'Go on.'

'Sure you won't help me with Grenville, Johnny?' There was a pleading note in his voice now. A big man whining because he wanted out. A frightened man, wanted for murder ten times over and trying to find a way around it.

'Keep talking.'

He shrugged his shoulders. 'O.K. Johnny. I knew this dame was going to be knocked off. Callen gave the order. 'Don't

ask me why he wanted her out of the way.
Maybe she was getting in his hair. Maybe
she knew something and was going to
squeal to the cops. All I know is that the
order went out a couple of days ago. They
tried then but somehow, it came unstuck.
They only managed to get her last night.'

'Who did the job?'

'A guy named Torrens, Sid Torrens.'

'Where can I find him now?'

Vitelli rubbed his chin where I had
slammed him hard. He eyed me narrowly.
'You going to get this guy yourself,
Johnny? If you've got that idea, be careful.
You'll need that gun of yours and more
besides. He's a killer.'

I believed him, but I didn't say
anything. I waited for him to go on. I
knew Tony Vitelli. A hardened killer, but
with a flair for talking if you could only
get him started and give him the
encouragement he needed.

'He's hiding out a few blocks from
here. I'll take you there if you like.'

'No go, Tony.' I shook my head, smiling
tightly. I knew the kind of man this
hoodlum was. If he thought there was one

chance in a million of taking me unawares, he would jump at it. I could see by the glint in his eyes that he wasn't quite as scared as he wanted me to believe.

'Suit yourself. I'll give you the address if you want it that way.' He looked sullen as if everything was not going the way he had planned it. There were little beads of sweat popping out on his forehead. He scribbled quickly on a piece of paper, then handed it to me. He looked uncomfortable.

'Callen will kill me if he finds out about this,' he said harshly.

'That's your trouble.' I motioned him back over against the wall, turning round with his face to it. Then I hit him expertly behind the left ear with the heel of my right hand and he slumped forward at my feet without a murmur. I didn't want him running to Callen with the news of my destination until I was ready for them. If possible, I wanted a little while with this guy Torrens before anybody butted in.

I reached my car in a hurry, slipped behind the wheel and took off. Maybe the bar-tender wouldn't bother to take a look in the corridor for a little while, maybe, he'd go right away. Whatever he did, time was running short.

I found the address ten minutes later. It looked small but well-kept. Not the kind of place I would have expected a killer like Torrens to own. Maybe that ought to have warned me right away, but it didn't. I stopped the car, got out and knocked on the door. There was no answer. I had expected none. Without waiting, I pushed the door, found it unlocked, and stepped inside, easing the Luger into my right hand, the safety catch off. It was time to face up to the trouble which I felt lay in store for me today. Sid Torrens. Exposed killer. For all I knew he might be lying in wait for me in one of the rooms, crouched behind a door, a gun in his hands.

I opened one of the doors swiftly, peered inside. The room was empty, the furniture neat and tidy. A little warning bell was ringing at the back of my brain, but I failed to realise what it meant or what it was warning me against. I knew the ruthless edge of cruelty that was in

Tony Vitelli. He had seemed just a little too free with his information, even with a gun on him. I had expected him to put up more of a fight than that, but he had backed down unexpectedly.

Something moved behind one of the other doors as I walked noiselessly over the carpet. Cautiously, I pushed it open, then kicked it hard so that it slammed back against the wall inside. Going inside, I jerked the gun around to cover the guy who sat on the bed, in the act of pushing himself up onto his elbows.

He was a weedy looking character, not the killer type, but you could never be sure. I watched him carefully as I eased my way around the end of the bed. If he guessed why I was there, he might try anything.

'Sid Torrens?'

'Yes.' There was fear and astonishment on his face. He looked like a man trying to figure out things which were beyond his comprehension. He leaned forward with a jerk, his face twisting, his mouth working.

'Tell me what happened last night.'

'Last night.' His glance wavered to the gun in my hand and the muscles of his face were working overtime. I could see that he was getting scared. I steadied the gun and applied a little pressure. The sweat popped out on his face again and he brushed it away with the back of his hand. 'I don't know what you mean. Who sent you here?'

'That isn't important. Somebody killed Caroline Lomer last night. Pumped half a dozen slugs into her from close range. I had it figured that it might have been a mob killing and you're the trigger guy according to the information I've been given.'

'That's a lie! In God's name, I don't know anything about a murder.'

His glaze kept flickering from my face to the gun in my hand and then back again.

'The finger has been put on you, Torrens,' I said, half-believing him. I seemed to have drawn a rotten break, but I had to make sure. 'Stand up!'

He swung his legs to the floor and stood up. Carefully, I checked for weapons, found nothing. He was still scared and I wanted to know why. If he'd made any attempt to go for a gun, I would have slugged him, probably killed him; and he knew it.

'O.K. You're clean. But you're scared. Going to tell me why?' My words sound as if they had been made of glass, brittle, ready to shatter in his face.

'I don't know who told you I was the murderer.' His words tumbled out in a torrent from shaking lips. This guy was plain scared, I thought, scared spitless, and not only because of the gun on him. There was something more to it than that. Something I didn't understand just then, but which I knew I would have to understand before things went much further.

'I knew Caroline Lomer slightly. I'll admit that. But I hadn't seen her for almost ten years. I swear it.'

'But you knew that somebody wanted her dead.'

'No.' There was the same taut, frightened insistence. He stood tight and tensed, a little man with a fear inside him which you could feel as if it were electric. 'As far as I know, there was only one man who might have wanted to kill her, who hated her like he hated the rest of us enough to kill us.'

'The rest of you?'

He ran his tongue around his lips and made a helpless little gesture with his left hand. I saw him watching me furtively, still not sure of me. For all he knew, I too could be one of the hirelings of the Underworld bosses, probing into everything he knew before killing him. He seemed like a rat running around in a box, not knowing which way to turn, trapped with his back to the wall. Perhaps he'd had second thoughts on how much he was going to tell me. He may even have had me figured as somebody in league with the cops, but I didn't think so.

Then his gaze flicked sharply to something over my shoulder and I knew instinctively that something was about to break. I half thrust against him, to hurl him to the ground, but I was seconds too late. He went down, sagging to his knees, falling heavily against me, but he was dead before he hit the floor. There was a black circular hole between his eyes and a vacant look on his thin, pinched features.

Somewhere down in the street, I heard a car start. Anger, such as I had scarcely ever known before, took me by the collar and shook me hard. Dimly, from the window, I caught a glimpse of the car disappearing around the far corner. It was a big black Cadillac, like those which the Organisation used whenever their hirelings carried out their orders. No point in trying to catch up with them, or even to tail them. They would have vanished into the maze of traffic long before I got to the street.

I went back to the body of Sid Torrens lay slumped against the wall. He wasn't going to tell me anything he knew. There was a sharp taste in my mouth. I had an idea now of how I had been used. They had intended to kill this guy Torrens no matter how it was done, but they had carefully chosen me as their killer and unwittingly, I had almost fallen into the trap. I swore savagely. I wanted to kill them for the trick they had played on me.

Of course, Vitelli had been in on it all the time. It had been a play on his part, pretending to be scared, to want out of the Organisation. She had been briefed well for his part. He had me fooled all the way along the line. The big-shot, acting scared, thinking all the time what a big-trusting fool, Johnny Merak was; the guy that Grenville had chosen for this job because he knew all of the mobs' methods.

I moved a little to one side to take another look at the dead man's face, then shook my head and stood up. What was the point in standing there looking at him? I didn't want to look at a man I had seen killed.

I got out fast. Unless I missed my guess, the cops would have been tipped off about the murder within seconds of it having been committed and they'd be on their way already, sirens wailing, ready to pick up Johnny Merak on suspicion of murder. I'd have a tough job talking my way out of that one. They'd be able to bring forward plenty of evidence to show that I'd been seen talking to Tony Vitelli, a well-known killer and the barman in the Golden Horseshoe would willingly testify to the fact that he had heard Vitelli give me the address where I might find Torrens.

Sirens were wailing a dismal dirge as I swung the Merc around the corner and headed back to the Office. I needed time in which to think. Events were happening a little too fast for me. Two murders in as many days, one of them in front of my eyes. I felt urged into activity by a new anxiety. Torrens, before he had died, had said that there was one man who hated Caroline Lomer, himself, *and the rest* enough to kill them.

What did that mean? It seemed highly likely that he had been killed because of what he might have told me. They hadn't trusted me once Vitelli had given me the address where I might locate Torrens. Wanting him out of the way, playing me for a sucker, they had sent me to kill him. But they had to be sure and it was possible that here, they had overplayed their hand. They had killed him using a silenced weapon, possibly the same weapon as that used to kill Caroline Lomer.

That wouldn't be difficult to check. But of one thing I felt reasonably sure, Vitelli wasn't the killer. That dark, shadowy figure still remained in the background. The nearest I had got to him yet was the faint plop of a silenced weapon and a car heading away into the distance.

The Office was empty when I arrived. Dawn was nowhere around. I poured myself a stiff drink and drank it slowly. There were a lot of things which still did not add up, but there was a faint pattern beginning to show among the apparently disconnected facts. The biggest piece of the jigsaw, the most important piece on which the final picture was based, was still missing, still out there somewhere in the city.

A killer on the loose. A dangerous man who had not yet finished killing.

3

Killer on the Prowl

It was the big fix. Indirectly, of course. These boys were trying to play it very clever. The orders were going out and I could only get a vague glimpse of the overall picture. I wondered again whether to contact Grenville. Perhaps it would be better if I put him in the picture. Getting to my feet, I walked over to the phone, put out my hand to lift the receiver from the cradle, only to have it ring in my face.

I let it ring for a couple of seconds, then lifted it and heard Grenville's voice at the other end.

'Johnny?'

'That's right, Harry. I was just on the point of calling you.'

'Something happened, Johnny?' There was a taut insistence in his tone that sounded clearly even over the phone.

'If you can call a second murder

something — yes.'

'Murder?' The voice never wavered. It was almost as if he had been expecting it.

'A guy called Torrens. Ever heard of him?'

A pause. I could almost hear the wheels ticking over in his brain. Then he seemed to shake his head at the other end of the wire. 'No. It doesn't click with me. Should it?'

'I'm not sure. I had the lead that he was the killer. I went to check with him. He was scared spitless, sweating ice-cubes when I got to him. Tried to tell me something — I figure it must have been important — because the next thing I knew somebody had used a silenced revolver on him from the window.'

'Did you see who it was?'

'No luck, I'm afraid. By the time I got there, all I saw was the tail end of a car vanishing around the corner of the street. Torrens was dead when I got back to him. But there's something I'd like you to check once you get the body.'

'What's that, Johnny?'

'Check the bullet that killed Torrens

against those which you dug out of the Lomer dame.'

'You reckon they might be fired from the same gun?'

'It's a chance. I figure the killer made his first big mistake this morning when he killed Torrens. Although I still don't see where either Torrens or Caroline Lomer fit into the picture. I can't find any trace of a connection between either of them and the Underworld Organisation. The only thing they had in common as far as I've been able to find, is that they were both scared of being killed. This guy Torrens had himself tucked away in some back room where it would have taken a month of Sundays to locate him unless you knew where to look.'

'That's the point I've been trying to figure. Just how did you know where to look? Murder seems to pop up every-where you go, Johnny. What the hell are you — a magnet?'

'I got a call last night from some guy who wouldn't give his name but reckoned he had information on this Lomer killing. I met him at nine this morning. He was a two-bit killer named Vitelli — '

'Tony Vitelli?'

'That's right. How the hell did you know?'

'Never mind that for the moment. Go on.' An urgency in the other's voice now as if something had just clicked into place in his mind.

'He gave me the low-down on this fellow Torrens — claimed he was the murderer and that I'd better keep my gun handy in case of trouble. Told me not to let the guy's appearance fool me. Then he gave me the address after a little persuasion and I went along.'

'I guessed there might be something like that at the back of it all.'

I felt like a kid groping around in the dark. A couple of minutes back, I thought I knew some of the answers — now I wasn't sure. I wasn't sure of anything any longer.

'What's on your mind, Harry?' I asked finally.

'This guy Vitelli. We found him less than thirty minutes ago.'

'You picked him up. That's fine. Maybe

he can answer a few questions. Where is he — at Headquarters?'

'Wrong to both questions, Johnny.' My heart did a double flip. Somehow, I guessed what was coming before he spoke. 'Tony Vitelli isn't at Headquarters and he won't be answering any more questions. We found him in his car at the bottom of a ravine ten miles from the city limits. He's in the morgue and he's dead.'

I stood by the phone for a long moment. In a way, I'd expected it, but not so soon.

'You still there, Johnny?'

I swallowed. 'Yeah, I'm here, Harry. Just trying to figure things out. Looks as though that's my only lead finished.'

'Better get down here right away. I'd like to talk with you. This thing is building up to explosion point.'

'I'll be there inside fifteen minutes,' I said in a lifeless voice.

I put the receiver in its cradle. It seemed as though I was being beaten to the punch all along the line. Somebody big was behind all this, the big machine was checking everything issuing the orders. I began to feel finished.

Dawn came in a couple of minutes later, threw me a swift, inquiring glance as she lit herself a cigarette.

'Something wrong, Johnny?'

'Plenty. A guy gets himself killed right in front of my eyes and I couldn't do a damned thing about it. Now my only lead, a killer by the name of Vitelli is found in an auto smash out of town.'

'Dead?'

'As dead as any guy would be after hitting a ravine at seventy with his car crushed like paper around him,' I said bitterly.

'What about Grenville?'

'I'm on my way to see him now. Care to come along for the ride?'

She nodded, stubbed out the cigarette and preceded me along the corridor, out into the sunlight. The fog had lifted completely now and it was just another cool November day outside. Little disconnected ideas were flitting about inside my head like flies as I slipped behind the wheels and gunned the Merc into the stream of traffic, heading uptown. How big was this man behind the killings? What motive could he possibly have? As far as I could see there was no connecting link between the two people who had been killed. Tony Vitelli was a different matter entirely. He had been killed to prevent him from talking at any time in the future. His death was an insurance policy on the killer's life. He had played his part well and now his usefulness was finished.

If only I had been able to get to Vitelli before he had been killed, it would have helped a lot. Somehow, I would have made him talk. Knowing the identity of one's enemy always helped.

Grenville was in when we arrived and the secretary behind the desk in the outer office, ushered us through with the minimum of formality.

He gave us a brief nod, motioned us to a couple of chairs. There was no smile on his face and his lips were compressed into a grim, hard line. 'I've got a couple of men checking back through the files to see if they can dig out anything on either Caroline Lomer or this guy, Torrens,' he said briefly, lighting a cigarette. 'I doubt whether they'll come up with anything, but it might pay off. Anyway, at the moment, there isn't much else we have to go on. We know about Tony Vitelli, but his death won't help us much. We may be able to prove murder, but it's going to be pretty rough. At the moment it looks like an accident or suicide.'

I shook my head slowly. 'A guy like Vitelli doesn't drive himself off the road and into a sheer drop of two hundred feet.' I said. 'And the state of his mind was anything but unbalanced when I last saw him.'

'Sure, Johnny. You and I know it was murder to stop him from talking. But we'll have a job proving it. I'm keeping it out of the papers at the moment. It's only a hunch I'm working on, but I figure if we let them think that Vitelli might still be alive, it may force their hand.'

'Did you check the bullets taken from Torrens and Caroline Lomer?'

'I'm having that done right now. Care to come along and take a look. It shouldn't take long.'

We followed him along a narrow passage, up in an elevator, and then along another, shorter corridor, through a glass-panelled door, into a room lit with brightness. The light made an edge of brilliance for Dawn's face as we went inside. The two men working at the bench glanced up briefly as we entered, then went back to their work. Grenville walked across to one of them, stood quietly behind him, at his shoulder.

'Have you come up with anything yet, Pete?' he asked softly.

'Just ready to check them on the screen if you can give us a couple of minutes.'

'Fine. We'll wait.'

Five minutes later, the room was in darkness, a cold, almost antiseptic darkness which, for a moment, made me unaware of the others around me. Then someone switched on an actinic light and the square roll of canvas at the far end of the room was picked out in dazzling white. I waited. This might be the first lead we had, something real to base any further investigations on.

The images of the two bullets showed

clearly on the screen. One of the technicians stepped forward out of the shadows at the side of the screen with a slender pointer in his hand. He prodded the canvas.

'As you'll see, the marks on both bullets coincide when the images are superimposed upon each other.'

As he spoke, the guy with the projector did something which brought the two images together. The lines on each overlapped, slipped over each other, checking in every respect. There was a moment's silence, then the lights went up and I realised I was sitting forward on the edge of my chair.

Grenville let out a long sigh, turned to look at me. 'Just as you figured, Johnny. Where do we go from here?'

I shrugged. 'I only wish to God I knew. The one big lead we had is lying back there in the morgue on a marble slab. He could have told us. There might be another lead, but it could be dangerous. Vitelli was working for a big-shot named Callen. It might be possible to get something through him.'

'Harry Callen?' asked Grenville.

'The same. Sure, I know he's thought of as a dependable, solid citizen of the community. But there are some of us who were in the rackets, who really know him. He's one of the big men in the business.'

'Do you want any kind of protection, Johnny?'

I knew Dawn was watching me with worried eyes as Grenville asked the question and I knew that I would have to give the wrong answer as far as she was concerned.

I shook my head, not looking at her. 'That wouldn't help, but thanks for the offer just the same. I'll have to do this alone. I know these men, I know how they work and where to locate them. If I went in there with any help, they'd smell a cop a mile away, before he loomed above the horizon, and we'd get nothing out of them.'

'O.K., Johnny. Play this thing your way if you want to. As far as I'm concerned, you've got a free hand in this. But watch yourself. I don't want to have to investigate your murder, you know.'

'Sure, I'll watch my step.' I got to my feet and followed the others out. Behind us, the two technicians were busy putting their gear away.

Back in the Office, Dawn looked at me a little accusingly. 'Why do you have to do these crazy things, Johnny?' Her voice sounded as though a little bit of hope had been beaten to death inside her mind. 'Why does it always have to be you to go knocking your head against this hard core of hoodlums and killers? One day, you're going to find yourself in the same position as Caroline Lomer and the others.'

I took her by the arms and made her face me. 'Somebody has to go out there and do the dirty work, Dawn, or the world will never be a clean place to live in. I know what it's like. I know the way these hoodlums work. If I don't stand a chance, I couldn't expect anybody else to go in there.'

'I suppose you're right, Johnny.' She leaned against me for a few moments so that I could feel the smooth warmth of her. 'Can I do anything?'

'Sure, Dawn. I want you to check back

through the files and all of the newspapers you can get your hands on. See if you can find anything to link Caroline Lomer with Torrens. There has to be something or this whole business doesn't make sense. The sooner we find this out, the better. Because if we don't, he'll kill again — and again. The man's either a maniac, or he's got some deep-seated motive, some hatred burning away inside of him, that we haven't discovered yet.'

* * *

At the first three likely places, I drew a blank. Nobody had heard of Harry Callen, or at least, they denied having known him for their own good health. It figured. Whenever a guy comes around asking leading questions about a big-shot like Callen, he's either a cop or somebody from a rival outfit in one of the other cities, Detroit or Chicago, and either way, it doesn't do any good to talk. So they shut up like clams and I didn't dare ask too many questions for fear of finding some big gorilla with a .38 in his fist waiting for me whenever I left.

At the fourth place, I struck lucky. The parking lot outside the eating place, which I knew had been frequented by some of the big shots in the past, was almost filled. Cadillacs were in the majority, but there were a couple of creamy white Lincoln Continentals lined up there with the others. The Mercury looked kind of out of place among that gathering, especially with the paintwork scraped off one side and the fender bashed in a little after the argument with the wall a couple of nights back. I parked near the back of the lot, slammed the door, and walked slowly into the bar. It was cocktail time now and the room, with the long, wide glass window overlooking the bay, was busy. I found a seat at the bar and ordered a rye on ice.

The first drink tasted fine, but only made me realise how hungry I was and how long it had been since I had eaten a proper meal. I determined to remedy that at once, and leave the job of looking for Harry Callen until later. That was what I intended to do, but events took another course.

Less than a minute after I had found myself a table in one corner of the room, a couple of ugly-looking guys sidled up to me and sat down. They looked tough and efficient.

'Hello, boys.' I said cheerfully. 'Looking for somebody?'

The larger of the two nodded. 'We hear you've been around several joints asking for Callen.' I could hear the gravel grating in his voice. No expression on his face which looked as if it had been chiselled from a solid block of granite. There'd be a .38 in his jacket pocket and another snuggled up under his arm.

'So?'

'Just between us, what do you want with him?'

'I'd just like to have a talk with him. I might be able to help him. It seems the cops have some information which might give them a lead on him. That could be bad.'

The other's face never changed, the dark eyes never wavered. I relaxed slightly. There was no immediate physical threat here. Callen was no fool. He would want to know exactly why I was seeking him out before he decided whether to dispose of me. When that happened, it would be done quietly and discreetly, without any fuss. A big man like Harry Callen could not afford to have any violence connected with his name, no scandal whatsoever.

'You ready to come with us, quietly. Or do we have to make you come along?'

'Sure, I'll come,' I said quietly. I thought I detected a faint look of disappointment on the other guy's face, but it faded quickly. 'So long as we go straight to Harry Callen. He might not like it if you did anything foolish.' I saw the other flush under the implied threat and his knuckles showed white on the top of the table. He waited until I had finished my drink, then lumbered heavily to his feet, scraping back his chair.

I fell into step between them as we made for the door. A couple of guys gave us a funny look, then turned their heads away quickly, probably realising what was happening and not wanting any part of it. I hadn't recognised either of the two strong-arm men. For all I knew, they weren't from Callen at all. But that was a chance I had to take. I knew I wouldn't get the opportunity to use the .38 in my pocket, so I kept quiet and sat in the back of the black Sedan which stood close against the front entrance. One of the hoods got in behind the wheel while the other crushed into the rear seat beside me.

'You don't seem to be taking any chances,' I remarked.

The guy beside me froze me with a warning look. He slammed the door and we moved off. I had a brief glimpse of my Mercury standing alone in the parking lot, then we were out into the main thoroughfare cutting through the lanes of southbound traffic towards the outskirts of the city.

The house, when we reached it, was set well back from the road, shaded from view by a thick fringe of trees which grew up, tall and straight on either side of the massive stone-pillared gates. The car drove straight through, along a wide gravelled drive, before turning and stopping in front of the porch.

The house itself was little short of impressive. I felt no surprise. It was the sort of house that nobody could afford to buy unless he was in the two-hundred thousand bracket, which Harry Callen evidently was. There were three cars parked in front of the porch and another in a garage at the side of the house.

'Inside,' snapped one of the gorillas as I got out of the car. He lumbered up behind me, very close. I thought about the gun in his pocket, but knew that he would be able to make a good account of himself without the gun. At the moment, I didn't feel like making him prove it.

I moved in front of him, across the porch and into the house. We came into a wide living-room which looked almost as vast as the Country Hall. It was luxuriously furnished and I guessed that the painting around the walls must have cost somewhere close to a cool million bucks.

But it wasn't the painting which first

took my interest. It was the guy sitting behind the writing desk in one corner, close to the windows. It was hard to believe that this guy was sheer poison. He looked smooth and suave, about forty-five, wearing a loose-fitting robe of brilliant scarlet which somehow seemed to clash with the rest of the decorations in the room.

'Heard you were out looking for me, Merak,' he said smoothly.

The two troopers took up their positions unobtrusively on either side of the door. No chance of getting out that way if the time came when I had to make a run for it.

'That's right,' I said, forcing myself to speak casually.

'What's on your mind?' Of course, he had guessed that there was something more to this than just a guy wanting to give him some information. He knew me by sight, and possibly by reputation. He must have known about my past, that I had once been in the same dirty rackets as those he headed and that I had broken clean with them. The big men had never forgiven me for that. They knew I was working on the other side, and I would do everything in my power to get them and put them where they belonged and sooner or later, they would make their move, to get rid of me. If Harry Callen was thinking along those lines at that particular moment, it did not show on his face. He seemed quite at ease, but with a couple of bruisers like those guys standing on either side of the door, ready to move in like a couple of steamrollers and smash me to pulp if I gave any trouble, a guy could afford to be at ease.

'I hear you've been having a little trouble during the past day or so.'

'Trouble?' The thin brows lifted just a shade. 'I'm afraid I don't understand the word, Merak.'

'Maybe not.' I shrugged and seated myself on the white couch in front of the writing desk. One of the gorillas took a step forward but Callen waved him back. Callen was smiling thinly, looking as if the answers to his questions didn't really matter. But that was an illusion which might have fooled a lot of guys, but not me. I knew Harry Callen of old. His brain was a photographic plate which took in facts and stored them coldly and precisely, so that a couple of years from now, he would be able to bring them all out in the open, every little inflexion of my voice, every little quiver in it.

He waited for me to go on, taking out a cigarette from a golden case and lighting it with a methodical, exaggerated care. He did not offer one to me and the omission was deliberate. As far as he was concerned, I was nothing. A little cog in some machine which he operated.

'I suppose you've already heard about Tony Vitelli?'

'Vitelli?' Again the questioning arch of the brows. 'Do I know the name?'

'You should, seeing that he worked for you.'

'You seem to know quite a lot, Merak. Possibly far more than is good for you.'

'Well, that's me all over,' I said, and I knew that to him the words and the way they were spoken, were deliberately insulting. 'It seems that Vitelli has been involved in some sort of accident out of

71

town. Ran his car off the road into a ravine. Pretty badly smashed up from what I heard, but the cops reckon he'll live to stand his trial.'

For the first time there was a flicker of something more than mere passing interest at the back of his eyes. He leaned forward in his seat and tapped the ash from the end of the cigarette into a slender tray. His lips tightened a little.

'He's still alive then?' Only for a second did his glance flick over my shoulder to the two hoodlums standing at the door. I noticed it instantly, but gave no outward sign. If Vitelli were still alive, that was the red alert signal to the men who had been entrusted with his slaying. I could imagine what would happen to the two hoods once I was out of the way.

'He was alive when I last saw him.'

'When was that?'

'Less than an hour ago. He was still unconscious, but the cops have got him locked away in one of the rooms at the City Hospital. No visitors by order.'

'Then how did you get in to see him, Merak?' Suspicion flared for an instant in his hard, steely voice.

'I'm working on this case. Or didn't you know that?' The other knew it, naturally, so I wasn't giving anything away when I had admitted it. 'They reckon he stands a good chance of regaining consciousness. If he spills what he knows to the cops, it might come hard on you.'

'Just why are you telling me all this, Merak. It isn't out of the goodness of your heart. I know that. You've got some other reason for it and I'd like to know what it is.'

'Sure,' I said, leaning forward. 'I want the name of the guy who killed Caroline Lomer and Torrens. That's all I'm after. What you do with Vitelli is no concern of mine. In my books, he's nothing more than a two-bit killer.'

Callen shrugged. His brain was working overtime, trying to figure anything else which might lie behind my visit there. He was a cautious guy, which was perhaps the reason why he had reached the position he had. But there were always the other bosses of the Organisation who could step in and smash him if they felt so minded. He wasn't the biggest by a long way. He held on to his power and position by sheer terror.

If Vitelli were still alive, then the chips were down for him. He would have to stop him from talking, from spilling everything. No excuses.

'So Tony Vitelli's still alive,' said Callen musingly. He blew a ring of smoke into the air and spoke through it, almost dreamily. 'It may be that he could make things a trifle awkward for us, but so could you, Merak, if you talked to the wrong people.'

'I've had plenty of time to do that in the past seven months if I'd wanted to,' I said pointedly.

'Of course. But that's no guarantee, is it? You see my position.' Smooth, purring talk from a killer. 'You could quite easily lead the police to me and that could make things very difficult for me.'

'Naturally. But I carry my own insurance whenever I go out on business like this.'

'Insurance?' There was a steely glint in the other's eyes now and his face seemed to change subtly.

'Of course. I like to think I'll get out of these places in one piece. That's why I always let somebody know where I'm going.'

'You're lying, Merak,' snarled one of the gorillas behind me. 'We weren't tailed here, boss.'

'Of course not. Nobody knows you're here, Merak.' Calleen was smiling smoothly now, completely on balance. 'You've no need to worry on one score though. We'll take good care of Tony Vitelli. Even if he is tucked away in the Hospital, we have ways of getting inside there.'

I knew that what he said was true. A nurse taking over from one of the other sisters. Somebody planted there by Callen or one of the other big men. It was all so simple. A hypodermic loaded with something else, something more sinister, and they could knock off anyone. Only in this case they would discover that there was nobody to knock off. It wouldn't be long before they found out that Vitelli was dead, after all.

I wondered whether I would get a

chance to go for the gun in my pocket. I doubted it, but I intended to make every effort. I knew only too well what happened to guys who crossed up the big men. Sooner or later, there came the inevitable pay-off. The Organisation could wait, patiently. Sooner or later, every account was settled, every score paid in full.

'You seem to be very anxious about this killer,' said Callen after a brief pause. His eyes watched me every second, not once wavering from my face. 'What's it with you? Why the sudden interest in this?'

'I just don't like to see anybody shot down on the street,' I said thinly. 'Any ordinary slaying, it's nothing to do with me. But I can smell a mob killing a couple of blocks away and this was one of them.'

The other's lips tightened. Then he smiled again. 'You're being extremely foolish, Merak. Don't you know when to stop? You've been riding us for long enough. I reckon it's about time we put a stop to you permanently.'

I sensed the two guys behind me,

closing in and tried to go for the gun, swivelling on the couch as I did so. I caught a brief glimpse of Callen's face watching me with a twist of sardonic amusement on his lips, then everything exploded in my face.

4

Date with Death

Being carried out of the room was something I didn't remember. It must have been nearly a couple of hours later before I woke up, stiff and sore with a lump on the back of my head as large as a pigeon's egg. After I got to my feet and looked about me, I felt stupid, but it figured. I ought to have known that a big guy like Callen wouldn't take any chance at all as far as his own security and reputation was concerned.

I guessed the place in which I found myself was a cellar of some kind. If it was inside Callen's house, it wasn't the part of it he would show to any of his guests. But it was the ideal place for keeping an unwanted guest until the time came for him to be got rid of permanently.

The gun was missing from my pocket, but I hadn't hoped to find it still there. I shrugged my shoulders and took a quick look around me. There was a pile of packing cases in one corner and the only light in the room came through a grilled window set in the wall just above eye level. I could see blue sky through it, but that was all. I knew instinctively, that even if I shouted until I was blue in the face, there would be nobody around to hear me.

I tried to figure out why Callen had put me down here instead of getting his hirelings to finish me off as he had promised. It didn't make sense, I decided, unless he wasn't as sure of himself as he wanted me to think, and there were more questions he wanted to ask before he was through with me.

There was the click of the lock on the door and it opened inwards. One of the gorillas came in, closed the door behind him and seated himself on one of the packing cases, one leg swinging idly. He looked a sitting target. Had all things been equal I might have taken the chance of rushing him, big as he was. Had all things been equal. Only they weren't and could never be, with that .38 in his rock-like fist, the barrel pointed straight at my stomach.

'May as well sit down and enjoy yourself while you have the chance,' he said pleasantly. 'Because you won't be able to much longer.' He laughed. An ugly sound in the stillness. It was the sound I would have expected evil to make.

'You reckon you're going to get away with this?' I said, looking him straight in the eye.

His lips curled back revealing tobacco-stained teeth. 'You think we won't, punk?'

'You'll be damned fools if you try it.' I forced evenness into my voice. 'I wasn't kidding when I said that somebody knew where I was.'

For a moment his eyes narrowed and I knew that my words had struck home. He was no longer as sure of himself as before.

'You're lying,' he snarled finally. But the barrel of the gun had wavered a little off target. Not much, but enough to make me think there was a chance of making this pay off if I could only make him still more doubtful.

I shrugged nonchalantly. 'Suit yourself,' I said. 'It's nothing to me. I suppose you've heard of a guy called Grenville?'

'Who hasn't. The Federal man in L.A.'

'That's right. He happens to be a particularly good friend of mine. In fact, I'm working with him as Callen knows quite well. Only he wouldn't tell you that. He reckons you're so dumb-brained you couldn't see the trouble that's heading for you even if you had a crystal ball.'

The other stiffened. For a moment his finger whitened on the trigger and I thought I had gone too far. Then he forced himself to relax and rumbled a harsh, grating laugh. 'You don't fool anybody, Merak. You're past fooling us. This is the finish for you.'

I thought fast. There wasn't much time if I wanted to get out of this mess alive. At any moment, Callen might give the order for me to be taken out for a ride and I knew too much of the methods of these hoodlums to expect to be alive at the end of it. A smashing blow on the back of the skull, a nice trip to the top of a convenient incline and then the brakes taken off the car and a bottle of whisky smashed in the back before I was sent off into death.

It was something I didn't relish, but unless I could get hold of that gun, I wouldn't stand a chance. There was a rush of thoughts flooding through my mind as I stood there, watching him. The minutes and the precious seconds were ticking away. Probably at that very moment, the other hood was busy getting the car ready for my last ride. Maybe they'd even be thorough and bring my own from the restaurant. Just to add the finishing touch to things.

The other guy was getting visibly nervous. He kept hunching himself forward onto the edge of the packing case as though expecting to have to take off at any minute.

'You think for one minute that Callen is going to let you live once you've taken care of me?' I said tauntingly.

I felt like a rat in a box, but I had one big advantage. I knew these guys. I knew how they thought, how they worked and how they felt. I could get behind their private fears and actions and see what motivated them; what pulled the strings inside and made them work the way they did. Looked at that way, it was possible to see that I had already got this guy on the edge of suspicion. If only I had enough time in which to plug away at his fears, to get him to loosen his tight guard for a single moment. That, I felt sure, would be time enough.

My life wasn't important to these men. They were big enough to buy and sell a dozen guys like me before breakfast. But now and again somebody popped up whom they couldn't buy, whom they couldn't figure; and I hoped that I was such a guy.

The gun in the hoodlum's hand wavered a little. His eyes flicked over me and I could almost hear the cogs of his brain, what little he had, whirring inside his head. 'What makes you think he'll try to get rid of me, Merak?'

'Simple, only you're probably too dumb to see it,' I said thinly. 'What happened to Vitelli when Callen was finished with him, when he figured that his usefulness was over? They fixed it so that he went over the edge of that ravine, tried to make it look like an accident or suicide, only you and I know better. We both know the kind of guy that Callen is.'

'That doesn't figure.' The other was shaken a little even though he tried not to show it. His face kept twisting and his eyes were no longer fixed on me, but continued to move swiftly around the room, almost as if he expected a dozen of Callen's other hirelings to pop up out of the walls and hustle him off before he had a chance to do anything about it.

'You're scared, anyway.' I kept up the pressure. 'Sure, he'll kill me. You'll take me for the usual ride, but even though I won't be coming back, I'll go with the knowledge that you won't be far behind me. Somehow, I don't think he'll make the same mistake twice. Besides, he won't be very pleased with you or your buddy now that he knows you didn't make a proper job with Vitelli. He's still alive and he's dangerous.'

'Damn you, Merak.' The other had pushed himself up onto his feet now, lurching towards me with a dangerous glint in his small, deep-set eyes. 'Just what are you trying to prove?'

The barrel of the gun was off target. Only by a fraction of an inch, it was true, but enough to give me the chance I needed. It was only a hundred-to-one chance anyway, so I had to take it whether I liked it or not. It was either that, or the last, lonely, one-way ride to death.

I decided to go out fighting, if it had to be that way. The hoodlum was less than three feet away, smiling thinly, his teeth shining, that dangerous glint still showing in his eyes. He was still a couple of feet away when I side-stepped smartly and hit him on the wrist. He yelped, more in surprise than pain, and dropped the gun. Now things had evened up a little, although after the beating I had received, the odds were still tilted in his favour.

I'd break my hands, or at least split my knuckles, if I tried hitting him on that granite-like jaw or forehead. Instead, I slammed a hard right into his throat, hitting him just below the adam's apple. He went over backward, onto his heels with the force of the blow, gasping for breath, all of the air knocked out of him, his breathing almost paralysed.

Crashing into him with my shoulder, I knocked him back against the wall, felt him give as I kneed him in the stomach. This was no time for finesse. I had to get out of this place — and fast. Any second now that door might burst open and another couple of hoodlums come in and hustle me off.

He broke my hold, hammered a short, jabbing left into my face. I went over backward, still hanging onto him, my foot in his stomach. It was an old cop trick without any of the trimmings. He flew over my shoulders and fell with a sickening thud against the opposite wall. We both came up, crouching, at the same time. I waited for his rush. He was breathing heavily, still unable to speak, blood trickling from his nose. He tried to bring the heel of his left hand up under my chin, but I smashed him away a hard right to the chest, then another to the pit of his stomach as he reeled back. His hands dropped momentarily to his sides, but it was the chance I wanted.

My fingers jabbed into his staring eyes, his teeth showed in a fierce grimace of agony and for the first time, a shrill bleat of pain burst from his swollen lips. He tried to pull away, to bring himself upright, but couldn't quite make it. My fingers, behind my back, closed on the length of piping which lay on top of one of the packing cases. It had been an oversight on somebody's part to leave such a lethal weapon lying around, as the thug soon discovered. He was halfway off his knees, clutching at me savagely as I brought it down with all my strength on the back of his skull. He leaned forward without a moan and kept on leaning until his face hit the dusty floor.

With an effort, I pulled myself upright. I was shaking terribly and my whole face seemed to have become swollen to twice its rightful size. If he wasn't dead, he would be out for a long time. I grabbed the gun, checked it, pulled off the safety catch just to be on the safe side, and opened the door. There was a flight of stone steps outside, leading upwards, twisting around a sharply-angled bend. Everything was silent. I went up them carefully, one at a time, found another door at the top.

This was half open. There was a swirl of pain in my jaw and cheeks and my ribs felt as though every single one of them had been either badly bruised or broken. A stab of agony lanced through me with every breath I took, but I forced myself to keep moving.

I began to feel that empty way inside. I could almost feel the hands of my watch grinding themselves around the circular face.

The room on the other side of the door was empty, but voices came from one of the adjoining rooms through another half open door. I tip-toed across the room, the thick, lush carpet deadening the sound of my footfalls. Harry Callen's voice, talking softly and confidentially. I glanced into the room. At first, he seemed to be talking to himself, then I noticed the curl of blue smoke rising in a lazy spiral over the back of the chair almost directly in front of me. It was impossible for me to see anything of the guy who sat in it, apart from a vague glimpse of the top of his head and the thick collar of his coat where it showed over the back of the chair.

Callen was saying quietly: ' . . . no use, the cops are bound to find out sooner or later. I tell you, it's too risky to keep on with it. Good God man, you've finished two of them so far, why carry this senseless revenge any further? It's only going to get us into trouble and with the election coming up in less than a couple of months, I've got to keep my nose clean. Nothing of this must be connected with me.'

I could feel the clammy wetness of my clothes as they clung to my tired, bruised body. I could feel the blood beginning to pound in my veins and behind my eyes. Those words of Harry Callen's throbbed inside my brain as I stood there not daring to breathe.

They could mean only one thing. The guy who sat in that chair, the guy I couldn't see, was the murderer I was looking for, the guy who had bumped off Caroline Lomer and Torrens. If there had been any doubts in my mind earlier, they were immediately dismissed when Callen spoke again.

'They can make it pretty hot for us if they start asking the wrong questions of the wrong people. Be smart. Let things be for a little while at least. You can't kill them all — or is that what you intend to do?'

'Naturally.' I tried to concentrate on that voice. It was one I had never heard before, but I felt sure that, a year, two years from then, I would remember it, even though it had spoken only one word.

'Then you must be crazy.'

The man in the chair stirred. I saw a hand reach out; a hand which sported a large emerald-green ring on the third finger. Callen pushed himself up out of his chair and waved an arm at the other. 'Steady. You know that isn't what I mean. But one man can't set himself up against the cops in this state and hope to get away with it without the protection of the

Organisation. We'll give you that of course,' he went on in a hurry, 'but you must realise our position. We can't afford any scandal at the moment in view of the coming elections. It's imperative that our candidate should get in. We've got more than five million dollars invested in him and that's too much to risk being thrown away.'

'Then what do you suggest I do?'

'Lay off for a couple of weeks until it's all by. Then we'll see what we can do. This guy Grenville who's on the case is a pretty smart guy.'

'And this other guy, the ex-crook turned do-gooder? What about him? It figures that he knows too much.'

'No need to worry on that score. He's been taken care of right now. Any minute and he'll be taken for his last ride. He won't bother us again.'

'Good.' The man in the chair chuckled and I felt a shiver run down my spine. That sound did things to me which I had never experienced before. It was the kind of chuckle I wouldn't like to hear on a dark night in a lonely street, even with a gun in my pocket.

I debated whether to step in and break up the little talk, to meet the killer face to face, but at that moment there was the sound of a door slamming somewhere further in the house and footsteps moving along the corridor outside, towards me. There was no time to be lost. Swiftly, reluctantly, I pulled myself away from the door and into a narrow alcove behind thick hanging drapes. I stood absolutely still. This guy might be out looking for trouble, on the other hand, he might be the other hoodlum coming to report to Callen that everything was in readiness for my future demise. I waited tensely as the footsteps moved past my hiding place, heard the nearby door open and then close. The sound of voices was cut off abruptly.

Giving them a couple of seconds in which to settle down, I skipped from the alcove and headed out of the room. Even with the gun, there was no guarantee that I would be able to handle the three of them, and any other there might be hiding around in the place.

As I had half suspected, my Mercury was ready outside the entrance, gassed up and ready to go. There was another car standing a couple of yards behind it with a guy sitting behind the wheel. He had his head half-turned as I came out, but had only time to let out a strangled yelp of surprise before the butt of the gun hit him soggily behind the left ear. He went forward over the steering column and stayed that way. Running for the Merc, I slipped in behind the wheel, started her up. There was blood on my face and I guessed I looked as big a mess as I felt.

My head was spinning madly and my chest hurt like fire as I gunned the Merc along the gravel drive, out through the stone columns of the imposing gateway and onto the main highway. I wiped the blood off my face with my handkerchief, but I wasn't thinking about my particular aches and pains at the moment. I was too busy wondering when those hoodlums back there would discover that the bird had flown and would come after me. They couldn't afford to let me get away with what I knew and once I hit the outskirts of L.A. their chances of intercepting me without causing trouble were almost nil.

I was trembling all over, shaking with suppressed nervous tension. I couldn't see any of the cars following me and it was a straight stretch of highway, for almost a couple of miles behind me. There was, of course, the possibility that Callen had taken an added precaution of having the cops set up a road block somewhere ahead of me. I knew, from past experience how closely men like him worked with the cops of half a dozen states. It was more than likely that he had the D.A. in his pocket too unless times had changed drastically and the people had elected a candidate of their own choice, an honest man.

I hit a curve at speed, felt the tyres claw at air for a moment, then settle back onto the road. In the mirror, I caught my first glimpse of the Cadillac as it appeared behind me. It must have been moving up fast, for it was less than half a mile away and closing the gap quickly. Whoever he was, that guy certainly knew how to handle a car. And the guy with him, as I had suspected, knew how to handle a gun. They were less than a couple of hundred yards away when he started firing. The first bullets fell short as I pushed my foot down on the accelerator giving the Merc everything she had. But an old car like that didn't stand much of a chance against these high-powered cars which were always kept in the peak of condition for times such as this. We were hopelessly outclassed. But there was one thing they probably didn't know. They didn't know that I had the gun. They clung onto my tail grimly, inching forward all the time.

Swerving madly, I slipped past a couple of heavy trucks which seemed determined to smash me as they came on in the opposite direction. I could almost feel the hunger in the minds of those guys in the car behind me. Professional men with a lifetime of experience in the slums of Chicago, Detroit, Los Angeles and any other place you cared to mention. Handpicked.

A bullet chirruped along the side of the

car, splintered the rear mirror, smashing it into little pieces. Another ploughed a neat furrow along the paintwork as I put the car into a sideslip. Those bullets were coming too close for comfort.

I rounded a long, shallow curve. The outskirts of Los Angles showed through the faint haze, directly ahead of me. Another mile and I stood a chance of giving these guys the slip. I felt a brief wash of bitterness. A hell of a lot could happen in a mile. I took a tight grip on the wheel, felt it slipping slightly in the sweat on the palms of my hands. Another sharp crack which I heard clearly above the hum of the tyres and the windscreen in front of me shattered. There was a rush of cold air in my face.

It seemed there wasn't going to be any future in which Johnny Merak would have a stake unless a miracle happened. There was more traffic in sight now, on both sides of the road, but nobody seemed to be taking any interest in us, not even the usual speed cops who happened to be hanging around looking for traffic offenders such as Johnny Merak with a couple of killers on his tail. Only that wouldn't wash. These guys had only to say that they were acting on Mr. Callen's order, that I was an escaped crook or something like that and it would be their word against mine, and I figured I'd never get the chance to call Grenville and have him vouch for me. I'd be bundled into that car long before then, probably with the blessing of the traffic cop and there'd be no escape a second time.

Less than half a mile ahead, a couple of heavy trucks, loaded with tuna fish for the nearby canneries, trundled ponderously forward, heading towards me. There was only a narrow lane between them and the nearside traffic and it was then that I got the idea. Johnny Merak bright boy. It was going to be a race with death, but I'd taken so many chances that day and they had all paid off, that I decided to go for broke.

I deliberately slowed the Merc until the Cadillac was less than twenty feet behind me. I could just see the guy sitting beside the driver. He stared straight ahead and if he had the gun in his hand, it was well hidden. Obviously, he wasn't going to take any chances with it so close to the city.

They'd be figuring on my motives for slowing like this. Once I started forward, they'd be on my tail again like a shot — and it was on that I was banking. They couldn't see the truck in front of me heading in the same direction. Not until the last minute did I swerve out into the narrow lane dividing the two. I felt the paintwork on the Merc being scraped off by the trucks as I slipped like an eel between them. The guy behind, gunning the Cadillac never stood a chance. I heard the harsh squeal of brakes, slowed and took a quick look behind me.

The driver must have seen the danger seconds too late for him to do anything about it. I caught a brief glimpse of his white face behind the windscreen as he pulled hard on the wheel but he never stood a chance. The gap between the two heavy trucks narrowed and caught the Cadillac between them, crumpling metal as if it were paper. There was a sickening crunch which I could hear above the shriek of brakes as the car folded in a blur of smashing steel. It slid between the trucks, torn in both directions, then leapt high into the air, turned over and over before it hit the far verge and went off the side of the highway.

It was all over in less than ten seconds. There was no more danger for the moment. The hoodlums had been so sure of themselves that they had sent only one carload of men to take care of me. I eased my foot off the accelerator. The Mercury slowed and I began to breathe more easily. Now that the immediate danger was past, I felt the sting of bruises and cuts on my body and my jaw felt tender whenever I touched it.

My mind twisted as I tried to figure out my next move. I reasoned I'd better tell Grenville what had happened. The big men would not wait before they started to move in on me now. L.A. wasn't big enough for me to hide anywhere and hope that they'd never give up now. I knew far too much about Harry Callen. I knew enough to put him into the penitentiary for several years on a dozen charges and this time, no matter how he had managed it in the past, we could make them stick. That was why it was so urgent for me to get to Harry Grenville. Grenville was competent, confident. I knew the scheming brain which lay beneath that cool and calm exterior. I knew that once he got his teeth into a job, he would never let go. My watch showed almost three o'clock. I wondered what Dawn was doing. There was always the possibility that Callen knew about her and was already putting into operation a plan to take care of her. Reaching the block which housed the Federal Agency, I got out, slammed the door behind me, and tried to disregard the aches and bruises. My face felt a mess and the secretary in the outer office stared at me as if I had just stepped out of some horror film.

'Mister Merak?'

'That's right, honey.' My face hurt every time I spoke, but I managed to force a smile. 'I'd like to see Mr. Grenville, if he's available.'

'I'll check whether he's in.' She spoke

hurriedly into the communicator on the desk. Grenville's harsh voice said something at the other end, then she looked up.

'Please go right in,' she said, nodding towards the door. 'He'll see you right away.'

I pushed open the glass-panelled door and went inside. Grenville looked up sharply, then waved me to a chair. He held out his cigarette case; lit the cigarette for me, then waited for me to start.

'Things are happening fast, Harry,' I said. 'Too fast for my liking.'

'You look as though you've been in trouble, Johnny.'

'Plenty of trouble,' I agreed. 'But at least, it's given me the answers to a few questions that have been worrying me for some days. Things are going to bust wide open within a few days and I've a funny feeling I'm going to be in the middle of them.'

'Harry Callen?'

'And the murderer we're after.'

Grenville leaned forward in his chair at that and looked interested.

'You know who it is?'

'It isn't quite as simple as that, I'm afraid.' I drew hungrily on the cigarette. It hurt my bruised jaw, but it was the only thing I wanted at that moment. 'I never saw this guy. All I heard was his voice. He was sitting in one of Harry Callen's deep chairs with his back to me. I had a gun but I had to move fast when one of the other thugs came in to report that everything was ready for my death ride.'

'I'm afraid you're running ahead of me, Johnny. You'd better start from the beginning. I may be able to follow you then.'

I started from the beginning, from the time I had been picked up by Callen's thugs and taken out to his country home. Grenville sat silent until I had finished, then nodded his head slowly.

'You realise what this could mean now, Johnny,' he said gravely.

I nodded. 'It means that by now, the whole of the Organisation will have been alerted by Callen. They'll stop at nothing to finish me before I can make any more trouble for them.'

Grenville looked worried. He lit another cigarette, flicked the spent match into the tray. 'I'll let you have protection if you wish, Johnny. You know that.'

'I know it. But it wouldn't serve any purpose. They mean to kill me and no matter how many men you put on to shield me, they couldn't stop the bullet of the fast car for ever. Los Angeles may be a big city, but as far as the Underworld is concerned there's no place they can't reach. No, thanks for the offer, but I think I'll have to play this as a lone wolf.'

'Suit yourself, Johnny. You know best as far as these thugs are concerned. But don't say I didn't warn you.'

He got to his feet and walked to the window, looking out, his back to me. After a while, I rose and joined him. The mist was beginning to form again, writhing in thin tendrils around the tall buildings. From Grenville's window, it was almost impossible to see the cars on the street below. Thousands of people down there, the majority of them going about their lawful business. But somewhere down there, would be the dangerous minority, whose only business was death and terrible mutilation and revenge.

And among them, unknown to me, undoubtedly bent on my demise, was a faceless man, a ruthless killer, known to me only by his deeds and his voice. I didn't like the idea of trying to find him alone in those milling crowds, but I was in a spot where I had to clutch at anything. It's unusually difficult to locate a guy like that before he spots you. Some guys might be able to do it; even Johnny Merak. But I figured I was going to be kind of lonely before I did.

5

A Date with Murder

Two hours later, I was on my way again. Dawn was waiting on the corner of Seventh and Twelfth. I stopped the car, waited until she had slipped inside, then gunned the Mercury away from the kerb. In spite of the attempt on my life earlier in the day, I still felt safer in the middle of the road. There, at least, you could always see death coming, even if it lay only a few seconds away. Among the crowds on the sidewalk, it could strike silently and swiftly and without warning.

I glanced at Dawn out of the corner of my eye. She lit a couple of cigarettes, slipped one between my lips.

'Did you find anything on either Caroline Lomer or Torrens?' I asked.

'Very little, Johnny. They both seem to have been nonentities in their pasts.'

'Just as I figured. Still, you'd better let

me have what you did manage to dig up. There might be something interesting that ties in with this case.'

'Caroline Lomer came to Los Angeles from somewhere back east almost five years ago.' She read from the small pad on her knee where she had made notes. 'Nothing earlier than that, I'm afraid. But here's the point that might prove interesting. When she first arrived here, she took a job as a waitress in one of the downtown motels, then graduated higher up the ladder of respectability and finally landed a job in one of the big department stores, a fairly responsible position. Then, less than a year ago, something happened. I couldn't find out what it was; but it must have been something pretty drastic, a turning point in her life.

'Without any warning, she threw up her job, one that paid her two hundred dollars a month, and went into hiding. There was a bit about her in one of the local papers, but beyond mentioning the fact that she seemed to have become a recluse, when she was still in her early twenties, it didn't elaborate any further.'

'Less than a year ago,' I mused. Little thoughts, like mice, were nibbling at my mind. It didn't figure. Why under the stars should a lovely girl like that, with everything in front of her, suddenly take it into her head to vanish off the face of the earth. The only answer was that she was scared of something — or someone. So frightened, that rather than risk her life, continuing as before, she had deliberately thrust herself into obscurity, into the shadows of Los Angeles, from which she had emerged for one brief moment when her body had been found on that lonely sidewalk in the November mist. The beginnings of an idea were forming in my mind, still nebulous, but crystallising more and more definitely when Dawn continued:

'That was the only connection I could possibly find between the two. Torrens came here two years ago from Arkansas. He seems to have been a model citizen like Caroline Lomer. No police record that I could discover. And yet, almost a year ago, he threw up his job at one of the big canneries and hid himself away in the city. I got his quitting notice from the firm if that's any use to you, Johnny.' She handed me the tiny slip of paper. I glanced at it casually, then slipped it into my pocket. It might furnish us with a lead; but at the moment, I was too preoccupied with trying to figure out why two people should take it into their heads to disappear around the same time, as if they were afraid for their lives. Almost as if the same event had occurred to both of them and they had been scared to be seen on the streets for fear of retribution.

Retribution!

It was a thought. It would mean a lot more checking before I could be sure, but it was something definite to go on.

I dropped Dawn outside the Office, sat still behind the wheel. She arched her brows at me. 'Not coming up, Johnny?'

'Not yet,' I shook my head. 'There's something I have to check.' I hadn't mentioned what had happened earlier. No sense in upsetting her. She'd find out soon enough.

'Watch yourself, Johnny. I've got a feeling this is going to develop into something nasty.'

'You can bet on that,' I said. 'Keep on checking on these two characters. Dig up every possible bit of news about them that you can. There's no way of telling at the moment whether or not it's going to be important.'

'Sure, Johnny.' She closed the door, stood on the side of the kerb as I pushed my foot down on the accelerator. She hadn't mentioned the mess my face was in. Even though I'd done my best to clean it up a little, the bruises and cuts still showed through. On the way downtown, I stopped in at one of the phone booths, called through to Grenville and asked him to put a couple of men on to watching Dawn. Whatever happened to me, would be because of my own foolishness, but I was determined that nothing was going to happen to her.

Grenville said he'd do that and I rang off, lit myself another cigarette and thought how nice it would be if I could just go into one of the nearby bars and drink steadily until I was past caring what happened to the world. There had been a time when I could have done that, but not now. I had the oddest feeling that more lives were hanging in the balance than I knew about, that this maniacal killer would strike again, and soon; in spite of what Harry Callen had said. Somehow, I had the idea that this guy didn't take orders from anyone, not even Callen; and that meant he was a pretty big shot in his own right, somebody at the top.

I felt a little shiver run through me as I stood on the sidewalk, glancing up and down the street. More of the terror and fear began building up inside me. Just who was this guy with the flashy ring and smooth, evil voice, whose back I had just glimpsed and who seemed bent on blazing a trail of death through the city. Somewhere around, in the slums and shadowed back streets there might be several more men and women of the twilight, consumed with the same kind of fear as had overtaken Caroline Lomer and this guy Torrens. Men and women waiting with a terrible fear of death.

The shiver came back even though I tried to shrug it off. I got into the car and sat behind the wheel for a moment, smoking, trying to think clearly. The pains in my body had subsided into a dull, suffusing ache which lay deep in my bones.

A couple of high-powered cars cruised by at the far end of the street, visible for a couple of seconds as they moved along the other highway. A little tingle went through me. There had been something terribly familiar about them, some singleness of design which I had seen many times before and which I had recognised instantly. More of Callen's men, moving in for the kill. The wheels of the Organisation were grinding now, moving slowly but inexorably.

The pick-up order would be out to every hood and killer in the city. Get Johnny Merak, dead or alive — preferably dead. That way they would be sure of me. I was becoming more and more of a menace to them every minute. At least two, possibly three of their men died since I had come into the picture and in every case, their deaths could be directly attributable to me. They wouldn't forget that. Had there been no other reason, that would have been sufficient for them to hound me down. But I could see the smooth, cunning brains of Harry Callen and this unknown killer behind it all.

I gave them a couple of minutes to get well clear of the district, then eased the car forward. Once I entered the maze of back streets, the rabbit warren that was downtown Los Angeles, I felt a little safer — but not much.

Slowly, I moved the car along the edge of the sidewalk until I reached the address which had been given me earlier by Grenville. There was no sign of the cops around and I guessed that they had picked up every scrap of information and evidence they could find and had left. The place looked dingy and down-at-heel, just the sort of place a woman would pick if she was trying to hide herself away from a fanatical killer. Nondescript. Like a thousand other places in Los Angeles, with nothing to distinguish one from the other.

Only this one was different. This was a very special place. This was where

Caroline Lomer had hidden herself away before she had been murdered.

It was getting dark as I parked the car. There was a woman standing outside with a tired face which looked as though it had seen better days. She eyed me curiously as I walked up the white, chipped steps.

'This where Caroline Lomer lived?' I asked.

'You from the police or the newspapers?' she asked suspiciously. It was a leading question. From the cops, she'd get nothing. From the Press, for a consideration, she might be able to recite the whole of Caroline Lomer's past history, embellishing it here and there as she went along. I was in no mood for this.

'My name's Johnny Merak,' I said. 'In a way you might say I'm working with the police. But I'm not a cop.'

She looked at me as if she expected me to walk off with the family silver, then sniffed. I dug down into my pocket and pulled out a couple of five dollar bills, turned them over in my hand. She glanced down at them briefly and there was a flash of greed in her eyes.

The bills were gone, snatched out of my hand and tucked away somewhere out of sight. 'Up there, on the second floor,' she said in a confidential whisper. 'The cops were here but they've been gone for a couple of days now, although they left instructions that nothing in the room was to be touched. But if you're from the police authorities anyway, I reckon it's all right.' She handed me the key and motioned me inside.

The room was on the second floor at the top of a flight of stairs. Hell, I thought, as I fitted the key into the lock, this dame couldn't have found a more down-an-out place if she had searched the whole of L.A. for it. The paintwork on the door looked as if it hadn't been renewed for ten years. The paper was peeling from the cracked walls and inside the room itself, there was that smell of musty dampness which tingled at the back of my nostrils. I threw open the window to let in some fresh air, then took a look around.

The cops would have been over the

whole place with a fine toothcomb. It was unlikely they would have left any clue of importance. But it wasn't anything like that that I was looking for. I was acting on a hunch. The hunch that a decent dame like Carline Lomer seemed to have been, would have wanted to keep something tangible which would remind her of the good old days, before she had been forced by some unknown circumstance, into this life which must have been completely alien to her make-up.

There was nothing in the drawers of the scratched bureau and the bed revealed nothing either. I began to look deeper. This dame must have been really scared if she had gone to all this trouble to hide anything which could have linked her with the past. I was beginning to feel more and more worried and defeated as darkness fell and I was forced to close the windows and snap on the light.

The light came from a single, unshaded bulb set close to the dingy ceiling. It gave very little illumination and threw a host of shadows. It made the room seem colder than before.

There was a noise at the door. Instinctively, I brought out the Luger, hefted it into my right hand, finger tightening on the trigger. The woman I had met at the bottom of the stairs stood there, blinking a little in the light. I felt sheepish as I stuffed the gun back into my pocket.

'Sorry,' I said quietly, 'I figured you might be someone else.'

'Were you expecting anybody, Mister? You seemed to be pretty scared having a gun out like that before you knew who it was.'

'In my business, you have to be careful.' I nodded towards the shabby bureau. 'Any idea where Miss Lomer kept her private papers?'

'Private papers?' She looked at me in surprise.

'That's right. Newspaper clippings, magazines. Everybody keeps things like that.'

She spread her hands in a universal gesture. 'She never mentioned anything like that. The police took everything from the drawers.'

'I can well believe that, but this isn't something they'd be looking for. I doubt whether they'd attach much notice to anything like this, even if they found it.'

'Well . . . ' The other ran her finger along her cheek. She looked dubious until I flicked out another couple of bills and pressed them into her hand. Her dubiety vanished in a single instant.

'She did have a small alubum if that was the kind of thing you were looking for.'

'Good. Where is it?'

'Downstairs in my room.'

'In your room?' I asked.

She nodded. 'Miss Lomer gave it to me two nights before she was — ' She broke off, then added lamely, 'before she was killed.'

'I see.' I didn't really, but there seemed nothing else to say. Why should Caroline Lomer give her album away to this woman and so soon before she had been murdered? It didn't make sense. Unless my hunch was right and there was something in it that she hadn't wanted anyone else to see.

I locked the door and gave her the key, then followed her to the room further along the passage. She rummaged around inside a chest of drawers and came up with a black album, tattered at the corners with what had once been a gold-leaf monogram on the front. I scanned through it quickly. Most of the cuttings inside were from way back, seven, maybe eight years.

'Is there anything there?' She peered at me shrewdly.

I pursed my lips. 'Difficult to say at the moment, I'll have to check through these cuttings. Do you mind if I take this with me?'

'Well . . . I'm not sure. She asked me specially to keep it here and on no account to allow it to fall into the hands of a short, thick-set man who wore a bright green ring on the third finger of his right hand.'

I began to feel that tight, empty way inside. More little bits of the puzzle were beginning to slot into place, but I still lacked any idea of what the final picture might look like. Always there was the image of this man with the emerald ring in the background. Occasionally, he would step into the foreground for a brief moment, and somebody would die.

'I'll return it to you if you wish,' I said, wondering inwardly whether I would be alive to keep that promise. 'Besides, you can see that I'm not the man she described and if you want to help to find the man who killed her, you can at least do this.'

Finally, she nodded. 'All right. You take it. She was a good girl, Miss Lomer. I don't know why anybody would want to kill anyone like her.'

'Neither do I at the moment. But I've got a few leads and this could be one of them. According to the police, she was frightened of someone.'

The woman nodded. 'She was frightened to death. But she would never say why. I asked her several times if there was anything wrong, but she wouldn't tell me. She'd shut up like a clam. Once, I remember she said that it wasn't good for me to know some things, that it could get me into trouble.'

'I see. Well, thanks for the help.' I went out, down the stairs, out through the front door, into the dark street.

I hadn't been expecting it then, but some sixth sense which never slept warned me there was something wrong. There was the brief sound of a powerful engine revving up at the end of the deserted street, of the car rushing towards me, the split second before I dived for the sidewalk, heedless of the punishing effect of the blow on my bruised body. Half-stunned, I still had the instinct to roll over, several times. Out of the corner of my eye I saw the spurting flashes from the side of the car as it roared past me less than ten yards away. There were no lights and scarcely any noise except the whining, jarring shrieks of the bullets as they spattered on the wall and hummed through the air where my head had been a moment earlier.

Something burned a red-hot line of agony along my left leg and there was the sound of glass shattering as a ricochet spat through one of the nearby windows. The car screeching around the corner was a protesting bleat of tortured rubber. Slowly, I got to my feet and stood shaking for a moment, pulling my thoughts into coherent shape. There was the smooth slickness of blood on my leg but the bullet had merely sliced through the flesh without nicking the bone.

Hell, but it hadn't taken them long to get on my trail, to trace me to this address and prepare a welcoming committee.

Somehow, I got behind the wheel of the car. I felt like a drink, but there was no time for that. At any moment that trigger happy hoodlum might come back to make sure he had finished the job and if he discovered Johnny Merak was nowhere around with half a dozen slugs in him, he'd put two and two together and start off on my tail again.

I stopped off at a phone booth in one of the more brilliantly lit streets, taking no chances of being caught on the hop again and rang Grenville.

The phone burred at me for several seconds before it clicked and I heard his voice at the other end of the line.

'Grenville.'

'Merak here, Harry,' I said. 'I've got some information here which may be important. Caroline Lomer left it with her landlady a couple of nights before she died.'

'Fair enough, Johnny. Glad you called in when you did. This is important too. Get over here as quickly as you can.'

'That may not be so easy,' I said harshly. 'They've tried to stop me again, this time a little more permanently. They were waiting for me when I came out of Caroline Lomer's apartment. They were playing for keeps. A sub-machine-gun.'

'You hurt, Johnny?' It was impossible to determine whether there was a note of concern in his gravelly voice or not. I didn't stop to think about it.

'Just a scratch,' I said. 'Seems I'm getting used to being shot at. There's an automatic alarm somewhere in my brain that warns me when there's something wrong.'

'O.K. O.K. Now get over here and try not to get yourself shot up on the way. Things are beginning to pop.'

'What's happened?' My first thought

was for Dawn. I hoped that the guys he had put on to watch her were efficient and competent. If this killer, or Harry Callen got their hands on her — I deliberately thrust the idea out of my mind. Thinking like that when it wasn't necessary, could slow down my reflexes to danger point.

Only dimly was I aware of Grenville's voice rasping at the end of the wire. 'There's been another slaying, Johnny.'

6

Justice and the Judge

'You still there, Johnny?'

My tired mind rolled over in my head, snapped back to full awareness.

'Yeah, I'm here,' I said slowly. 'You were saying something about another murder.'

'That's right,' he said. 'That's why I want you over here.'

'Any word from Dawn yet?'

'She's right beside me at the moment. Now for God's sake, get off that phone and get over here. When can I expect you — or would you rather I send out an escort for you?'

I smiled tiredly at that. 'It's O.K. I'll make it somehow, even if I have to fight my way through all of the hoodlums in Los Angeles.'

I replaced the phone in its cradle, pushed open the door of the booth and

124

stepped out into the cold night air. It smelled raw and moist in my nostrils. The pain in my left leg was still there making it difficult for me to walk. All I wanted to do at that moment was crawl away somewhere and sleep for a week, to forget everything that was happening.

The journey to the Federal block was uneventful. Either Callen's dogs had been withdrawn on the assumption that Johnny Merak's nine lives had finally given out and he was lying in a pool of his own blood on the sidewalk outside Caroline Lomer's apartment, or they had returned, discovered that I must have somehow survived, but had lost me by then once the trail had grown cold.

Pretty soon, I thought wryly, it was likely that Harry Callen would move in himself, see why his orders weren't being carried out to the letter, why Johnny Merak, the joker in the pack, was still alive and kicking when by rights he ought to have been laid out on a mortuary slab long before this. The showdown was looming up on the horizon, but it was impossible to guess how far or how close it was.

I stopped the car, got out, and climbed the steps to Grenville's office wearily. I felt a wreck, washed up. One beating and two attempts on my life were enough for one day, even for Johnny Merak. It was still early, but dark and the lights were on behind the office door. I knocked, then pushed it open as Grenville's harsh voice called to come in.

There were four people in the room. Grenville, sitting as always, behind his desk; Dawn, in the chair at one side, looking slightly scared and apprehensive; and two burly-looking guys standing one on either side of the door as I walked in.

Dawn got to her feet the moment she saw me and there was an expression of concern on her face. She took my arm as I walked forward.

'More trouble, Johnny?' said Grenville.

I nodded. 'I thought I told you that over the phone.'

'So you did. I'm afraid what's happened put all thought of that out of my mind.'

I settled myself into the chair as comfortably as my battered limbs would allow and took the cigarette he offered. Dawn lit it for me, sat down in the chair beside me. I grinned at her although the effort cost me more than I wanted to show.

'You're a fool, Johnny,' she said softly, so quietly that I might have been the only one in the room to pick out her words. 'But then, you always were.'

'Sometimes fools can tread where angels wouldn't dare,' I reminded her lightly. I turned to glance across at Grenville. He chewed at his lower lip. His fingers, on the top of the desk, were white-knuckled.

'Who's been knocked off this time, Harry?' I didn't mean it to sound callous, but these things had been riding me for so long that I was beginning to feel the first, faint stirrings of defeat inside me.

Grenville looked almost as defeated. His face was cold as he said tightly, 'Judge Samuel Buchanan was shot dead tonight at his home in Balboa Bay.'

'Judge Buchanan?' The name was

vaguely familiar, but beyond that I knew nothing of him.

Grenville nodded. 'I don't like bringing this up, Johnny. But you were on the wrong side of the law when Judge Buchanan had his hey-day in Los Angeles. He was a tough guy, sent many of the hoodlums to the penitentiary.'

'So you could say he was a man with plenty of enemies?'

'More than I'd like to have,' agreed the other grimly. 'But I've a feeling we might be able to pin this killing down to one man.'

I knew what was coming. Those other slayings had been of relatively unknown people, but from the sound of it, this Judge Buchanan had been a big guy in his time, a do-gooder who had refused to be intimidated by the Underworld and as far as they were concerned, all scores were settled, no matter how long it might be. The Underworld Organisation had a long memory and could afford to wait. Like an octopus, it spread its evil tentacles throughout Los Angeles and beyond, having contacts with similar organisations in most other major cities in the United States.

'What makes you so sure, Harry?' I asked tightly.

'The way it was done. It had the same look and feel about it as the others. Half a dozen slugs pumped into the body from close range. Obviously, the Judge had known the guy who'd killed him. But we'll soon be able to clinch it.'

'By matching the slugs?'

'Exactly. That way, we'll be sure.'

'And then it will all start again. I've got the feeling that we're knocking our heads against a brick wall and getting nowhere fast. Especially me.' I fingered the bruises on my jaw, winced a little as my fingers probed the tender spots. I felt as if my whole body had been pummelled and hammered unmercifully, so that every single inch ached with an exquisite torture that was worse than any pain.

I finished the cigarette and got to my feet. The rest had done me good. This time the room stayed put and didn't start tilting and swaying around me and the pounding, sick ache at the back of my temples was no longer as bad as it had been earlier.

I wanted to think things out coolly and quietly, but my brain wouldn't allow me to do so. It kept spinning around in circles, coming up with a hundred burning questions that didn't have any answers. I had the feeling that I was looking at only dark fragments of the picture, that the rest of it, the background and the central figure kept tantalisingly out of sight.

Going back to my seat, I said: 'What have we got so far?' I ticked the facts off on my fingers. 'We know there's one man at the back of all of these killings. That whoever he is, he's working hand in glove with Harry Callen, possibly giving the orders, although we can't prove that at the moment.

'We know that the only connection between the first two murders is that in both cases, the victims were scared of being killed, and I don't believe in foretelling the future. There was something more to it than that. They both dropped out of public life around the same time, about ten months ago. Now what happened then? Any ideas?'

Dawn shook her head and stared down at the floor. Harry Grenville shifted uncomfortably in his chair, hands clasped tightly in front of him. He looked straight at me, his mouth drawn into a hard line across the middle of his bluff features. The two guys lolling near the door tried to look as though they hadn't heard.

'Well?' I asked.

'Nothing that I know of, Johnny,' said Grenville miserably. 'I only wish I knew of something which might have a bearing on this. You seem to be getting pushed around at the moment with no returns for your trouble.'

'It may push them over the line. They made one mistake when the killer used the same gun for Caroline Lomer and Torrens. I reckon you'd find those bullets that were meant for me had the same trademark. Seems this killer is something of an egotist. He likes to leave his visiting card in the shape of a bullet.'

'How's that, Johnny?' asked Dawn.

'This guy is confident. Supremely so.

He's defying us to catch him before he's carried out his programme of slayings. That trait might be to our advantage if we can only swing it.'

'Just what are you getting at?' demanded Grenville.

'I've had plenty of opportunity to watch these killers in action. There are types and nearly every hoodlum and killer falls into one of these categories. This killer can easily be typed. I began to suspect it at the beginning. Now I'm sure.'

'Sure of what?' asked Grenville, leaning forward over the desk, resting his weight on his elbows.

'That he's insane. He has to be. He's a maniac, a man set on vengeance.'

'Vengeance.' Grenville seemed to be talking to himself. He nodded his head slowly. 'It fits! It fits!'

I sat still, watching him. The aches and pains were forgotten. Even the two guys near the door seemed to hold their breath.

'What's on your mind, Harry?' I asked.

'I'm not sure. It could be nothing. On

the other hand, it might be the answer we're looking for. If it is, then God help us if we don't move fast.'

He stood up quickly. Walking over to the filing cabinet near the far wall, he jerked it open and riffled through the papers inside, his face sharp and intent. When he looked up again, his face seemed to have changed, to be a little older than when he had looked away a few moments before. He pulled a file out of the stack of papers, carried it over to the desk and laid it flat in front of him.

'It all checks,' he said finally. His voice sounded tired and expressionless. 'I'd hoped for a break, but never anything like this.'

'You know who the killer is?' asked Dawn. Her voice was little more than a whisper.

'I think so. I only hope to God I'm wrong, but I don't think there's much chance of that.' He opened the dossier, ran his fingers aimlessly through the pages, not really seeing it.

'Who is it?' I asked tensely. The atmosphere in the room was electric.

Tight and tangible. I could have cut it with a knife.

'A killer with a streak of madness in him. A guy who wears an emerald rock as big as a pigeon's egg. Those were your words Johnny. That was your description of this man. Now, I'm going to put a name to him. Maxie Torlin!'

'Maxie!' I almost hissed the word. That voice I had heard speaking to Harry Callen. Now it all came back to me and I cursed myself for not remembering it before. But then, Maxie had been out of circulation for almost six years. Some said he was dead, that he'd been killed in a stabbing in the penitentiary. Others reckoned he was still there, serving a ten-year stretch. In the old days, you usually saw this guy Maxie Torlin around the flashier night spots of Los Angeles and Detroit. A keen-eyed, thin-faced man with no soul, a man who spoke with a gun before he used words. I'd run across him on occasions in the steam baths after a work out in one of the gymns or in the Flamingo night club, laying bets of several thousand dollars on the crap games or roulette. I'd known Maxie Torlin fairly well in those days, but only from a distance. He seemed to move in an orbit all his own, giving orders and knowing that they would be carried out.

There had been talk, of course. There always was with men as big as Torlin. Somewhere, sometime, there would always be another guy who'd hate his guts sufficiently to pluck up courage to do something about it. Nobody knew who had put the finger on Maxie. There had been plenty of times before when he had been picked up by the cops but nothing had been pinned on him. He had the D.A. in his pocket and a pretty smart lawyer to get him off the hook if the going became tough.

But this time, something more had happened. There had been evidence and the Federal Bureau had taken charge. Maxie hadn't been able to beat the rap and had been handed down six years in the State Penitentiary. It had made headlines at the time. But that had been almost five years ago. It couldn't possibly have had any connection with these slayings. And yet there was a tie-in somewhere if I could only see it.

'I thought you'd be surprised,' said Grenville. A low voice, dark eyes watching me.

'It could be,' I nodded slowly. 'That voice I heard in Callen's. It could have been his. In fact, I'm fairly sure it was. But if it is, we're up against a — '

'A maniacial killer,' said the other grimly.

I sank down into my chair again. The room seemed suddenly cold and quiet. 'Can we prove it. Up to the hilt, I mean?'

'I think we might.' Grenville flicked the switch of the communicator on his desk. There was a brief pause, then a tinny voice answered at the other end. It didn't sound like the dame I'd seen earlier in the outer office and I guessed she'd be away by now.

'Get me the file on a killer named Torlin. Maxie Torlin.'

The shrill, metallic voice said something. Grenville clicked off.

Less than two minutes later, there came a knock on the door and a slim, dapper guy entered. He laid the file on the desk in front of Grenville, hesitated a moment, then withdrew. Grenville lit another cigarette before opening the file, flicked the spent match into the tray.

Then he opened the file, read through it quickly, sucking in his cheeks as he smoked. Then he said, in the same lifeless tone he had used earlier:

'Max Torlin was sent to the State Penitentiary almost five years ago to serve a six year sentence on two counts. The charge of murder which was also brought against him was dismissed for lack of evidence. He was apparently given the maximum sentence on the counts where he was found guilty.' Grenville hesitated, then went on quietly. 'The Judge who presided was Judge Buchanan.'

'It's all beginning to make sense,' I said thickly. I stopped thinking about my pains and began to think about the murder. 'And this dame Caroline Lomer, and Torrens. They were on the jury that convicted Torlin.'

'That's right. They were.'

'Now we're getting somewhere,' said

Dawn softly. 'We know the motive and we know the killer.'

'It looks that way,' went on Grenville grimly. 'According to the file, Torlin was released from the Penitentiary about ten months ago after having time taken off for good behaviour.'

'And that was when these two went into hiding for no apparent reason. No wonder they were scared with a killer like Torlin on their trail. He swore he'd get those who sent him to the pen. But I figured he meant the guys who put the finger on him. I never thought for one minute he meant the Judge and jury at the trial.'

'You've got to remember that, whatever Maxie is, he isn't sane. Not as we would define sanity. He doesn't think the same way as we do. He lived for killing in the old days and I doubt whether he's changed now.'

I forced myself to relax. At least, I knew what we were up against. The killer had changed from something shadowy and half-mythical into solid flesh and bone. Had been given a name. Now we knew who we were looking for; but although that helped considerably, it didn't solve the problem. There were ten more people on the murder list if our theory was correct. It would mean tracing every one of them and giving them protection until we could catch Maxie Torlin. And that, in itself, wasn't going to be an easy task. He had been a big-shot in the old days, had run the Organisation as one of the top men. If he wasn't doing it again, he still seemed to be in a position to give orders and that undoubtedly meant that the Organisation was protecting him. Fight him, and we would have to fight the might of the Underworld. If he stayed within its confines, we would never get him unless we were prepared to go out and blast him from beneath a mountain of artillery. Somehow, I doubted whether even Grenville would consider that proposition.

No — there had to be another way. He had to be lured out into the open, to be trapped while he was out of reach of the Organisation.

'What are you thinking, Johnny?' asked

Grenville presently.

'Just trying to figure out a way of taking Torlin. It isn't going to be easy. Somehow, we've got to make him come out into the open.'

'First we've got to trace the other ten people who sat on that jury five years ago.'

'If you have the names there can't you trace them in the normal way?' asked Dawn.

I smiled thinly even though it hurt my lips. 'That would be routine under normal circumstances, Dawn. But you know what happened to Caroline Lomer and Torrens. They tucked themselves away so that Torlin couldn't find them. You can bet your bottom dollar that these other ten people have done the same. They'll be hiding somewhere out there in some out-of-the-way place, maybe not even in Los Angeles. We'd never find them in time.'

'But what about this man Torlin? How does he find out where they're hiding?'

'He has a better organisation even than ours,' said Grenville harshly. He climbed swiftly to his feet, returned the file to the top of the locker. 'You can be sure that he's been planning his revenge all the time he's been in Big Q. He'll have had men on the outside watching and following every one of these people. They'll know where they are at this very minute. They'll have been shadowing them night and day. You can't get away from a web of informants like that, no matter how hard you try.'

'There's just the chance that by now he'll have figured that we know who he is and the reason behind these seemingly senseless killings,' I said after a brief pause. 'He may also have reached the conclusion that we'll have sent out men to watch the rest of these people he's sworn to kill.'

Grenville looked puzzled. 'What are you getting at, Johnny?'

'Simply this. That he may decide these other murders can wait because he can always pick up the others whenever he likes, but that there's someone else who's more of a menace to him at the moment. If I'm right, there'll be eleven on his murder list and unless he's leaving it to Callen, I can guess who's at the top of the list.'

Grenville looked at me quizzically, brows raised into a straight, black line.

'Johnny Merak,' I said grimly. I wasn't afraid, but it was a hell of a feeling.

'You may be right, Johnny. I'll put things into motion right away, get a tail on these ten people if we can possibly locate them and also have that place of Callen's watched. It may give us a lead if Torlin's still there.'

'I hope you're right.'

'Meanwhile, Johnny. I think you ought to sleep on it. You're about all in and in no fit state to do anything about this case tonight.'

★   ★   ★

Back in the flat, I stripped down and went to work with hot water, then ice-cold water, finishing with a stiff rye. My face looked bad in the mirror with a couple of bruised patches and a deep cut on my cheek where the hoodlum's knuckles had laid bare the bone. Every bone in my body ached individually.

Putting on fresh clothes, I felt a little better. For the first time, I realised that I had had it in my power to kill Harry Callen and Maxie Torlin. They had been within killing distance of the hoodlum's gun which I had picked up after the fight. The thought was like having the bottom of my stomach drop out. I had a vivid mental picture.

Maxie Torlin, alive, with only one purpose in his life — finding and killing Johnny Merak and then getting down to the interrupted business of continuing with his plan of mass destruction. And as I saw it, he had plenty of reason for wanting me dead.

I felt nervous. If you've got to wait for somebody to come and make a play for killing you — sitting in the quiet of a flat isn't exactly the best place to do it. I thought about Dawn and began to wish that I was out of the whole rotten mess, that I could live the life other people seemed to live; ordinary, everyday people like the thousands walking in the street at that very moment.

Then, I thought about ten men and women, hiding in the twilight world somewhere, afraid to show their faces in the daytime for fear of collecting a bullet. Men and women scared to death, not knowing when death would come for them or in what shape, knowing only that it would come and it would not be long.

I smoked cigarette after cigarette as I sat there in the half-darkness, keeping well away from the window. There was no sense in taking unneccessary chances where these people were concerned. No point in making a perfect target for some trigger-happy gunman.

Perhaps they expected me to run. But I was staying here in Los Angeles until I had played this trick out to the bitter end. There would be no running. Not from a hate-crazed killer wearing an emerald ring who had already killed three times; not from a smooth-talking gangster who headed the organisation in this sector of L.A. I was about to light my sixth cigarette when the phone rang, jarring across the stillness. The sound made me nervous and did something to the tight muscles of my stomach.

I didn't think it would be a friend calling. Not at that time of night. As far as Dawn and Grenville were concerned, I was in bed, sleeping like a new-born babe.

It wasn't a friend, it was the big man and his voice wasn't smooth this time, it was harsh and jerky.

'Merak?'

I swallowed. 'That's right. What do you want, Callen?'

'Just a friendly talk, Merak.'

'Go ahead. I'm listening.' The line hummed for a few seconds, then Callen's voice came rasping over the wire again.

'You've been getting into my hair for some time now, Merak. I don't know why, but I don't like it. Just what it is you're setting out to prove?'

'I'm not sure what you're talking about.'

'Aren't you?' There was a hidden threat in the voice now, clearly audible to anyone who knew Harry Callen. 'You're in on this case with Grenville, the Federal man. But we've already established that, haven't we?' He chuckled ominously.

A little thrill ran up and down my spine. With an effort, I suppressed it. 'How's your boy, Callen? The guy who had to watch me down in that cellar of yours? I'm sorry I didn't appreciate your brand of hospitality, but I found it boring after a time.'

'Damn you, Merak. I've stood more from you than I've taken from any other man.'

'Including Maxie Torlin?'

It was the wrong thing to say to Callen. But it was necessary to get his response. 'You're playing with fire there, Harry. He's a killer in a class even outside yours.'

'What do you mean by that remark, Merak?' he snapped. I figured he was becoming a little rattled. The conversation was not going quite as he had planned. He had intended perhaps to intimidate me, but at the moment, things were going the other way. I laughed thinly.

'You know damned well what I'm getting at. Torlin is the guy behind these killings of the past few days. Now he's knocked off Judge Buchanan. That's where he made his fatal mistake even though he probably doesn't know it at the time. Because we've cottoned on to him. We know the names of all his intended victims. He'll find it more difficult to go through with his plan now. The whole of the Federal authorities is on to him. Better warn him that he'll be taken dead or alive. And you're too tightly meshed with him at the moment to be able to wriggle out of it, no matter how smart your lawyer is. Better get out of it now Harry, while there's still a chance.'

'For a guy who's not got long to live, you talk a hell of a lot, Merak. It's a pity that you know too much for your own health. I might have respected you for a lot of things if you hadn't been so keen to poke your nose where it wasn't wanted.'

'Fine words, Harry,' I sneered, trying to get him riled. 'But perhaps the boot is on the other foot. You've been a big shot for a long time now, pulling the strings, operating those puppets of yours, making them jump to your tune. But your time is coming to an end pretty soon.'

He seemed on the point of saying something else, then pulled himself up short. When he finally spoke again, his voice was carefully modulated, forced into evenness.

'You can't hope to fight a man like Torlin, Merak. You know that and deep down inside, you're scared spitless. He's coming for you, soon. Very soon.'

'Thanks, Harry,' I said, and calling him by his christian name was like spitting in his face. 'That's all I wanted to know.'

He said something unprintable, then the phone clicked and went dead close to my ear. I replaced the receiver, went over to the window, switching off the light first, before twitching back the thick curtains.

The street looked deserted, with two lights shining along its length. I scanned the scene quickly. Then I knew that it wasn't quite as deserted as it seemed on the surface. Less than twenty yards away, on the other side of the street, in the shadows, a tiny red glow showed intermittently. The tip of a cigarette, smoked by the man watching the house.

7

Attempt to Kill

Torlin hadn't been long in putting out his watchdogs to keep tags on me until he decided to carry out his threat. I retreated slowly from the window, allowed the thick curtains to fall back and switched on the dim light.

Point of decision. What to do now. Wait until Torlin made his move or try to beat him to the punch. I tried to figure out why Callen had been so anxious to call me, why he had let it slip out that Torlin was coming gunning for me. Knowing these guys as I did, it seemed unlikely that they would forewarn their victims and I didn't think that the two had fallen out. No — there was something more to this than met the eye. I thought fast. I didn't want to have to tangle with those hoodlums out there in my present bruised condition, but time was running short. I had counted on being given one night, but it didn't look as though I was going to make it.

Acting on an impulse, I phoned Dawn's apartment, but the phone bleeped in my ear for a couple of minutes and there was no answer. I then tried Grenville's place, but the result was the same. Slamming down the receiver, I poured myself another drink and sipped it slowly. It went down inside my stomach where it exploded into an expanding glowing haze. I began to feel a little better. A car went past and I waited for it to stop outside, but it kept on going, around the corner and away. That's the worst part of sitting alone, waiting for death, not knowing when or where or how it will come. There were plenty of ways for a fall guy like me to die.

Curiously, I didn't feel afraid for myself any longer. Perhaps so many things had happened that I was past feeling scared. And that, in itself, was a change for Johnny Merak. But I felt mad and helpless, not knowing what to do, and that was one hell of a feeling. I knew what kind of hoodlum killer Maxie Torlin was. A man with a big headache now that I knew his identity and the purpose behind his actions. He was the kind of guy who'd use every dirty trick in the book to get me, to stop me permanently. And for good reasons.

I went into the kitchen and made myself a cup of coffee, strong and black. I needed a clear head and the alcohol was blurring my mind too much. There was no sense in rushing into these things blindly. Perhaps that was what they wanted me to do; why Callen had called me and told me part of Torlin's plans; to throw caution to the winds and go storming out of the apartment into the first bullet that was waiting for me out there in the darkness. If that was what they wanted me to do, they were going to be disappointed. I knew far too much of their methods to do a fool thing like that.

Gulping down the scalding coffee, I went back into the room. My face and chest hurt and I felt as though I could sleep for months. But somehow, that little voice deep down inside my brain, kept telling me that now was the time for action; when they least expected me to do anything. I had the terribly urgent feeling that even at that moment, while I hesitated, big things were happening out there in the city, important things which I ought to know about.

See if you can find a way of fixing yourself out of this mess, Johnny Merak, I thought bitterly.

I put through another call to a guy I'd known from way back. Somebody on the inside, but who hated the big men like poison. If anybody could help me now, he was the man. The phone burred in my ear for several seconds before the receiver was lifted at the other end. Dimly, I could hear the sound of music in the background.

'Yeah?'

'Mike Spangler?'

'He's around someplace.'

'Get him for me. This is urgent.'

'Who shall I say's asking for him?' The voice at the other end sounded just a little too curious.

'Never mind about the name, just get him to the phone and I'll take over from there.'

'O.K. O.K. Keep your hair on. Just trying to be helpful, that's all.'

There was a faint clatter as the phone was laid down at the other end. I waited impatiently. It was some time since I had been in touch with Mike Spangler, safe-breaker, conman, forger and anything else that paid off handsome dividends without too much physical effort.

The sound of quiet breathing at the other end of the line, a pause, then Mike's voice, like gravel on a tin roof, saying:

'Spangler. Who's that?'

'You all alone, Mike?'

'Sure. That you, Johnny?'

'Right first time. Listen, Mike, there's no time for long explanations. I've got to have some information and I need to have it fast.'

'Sure, Johnny. Anything for you. Who's the guy?'

'You catch on fast, Mike. Ever heard of a big-shot called Torlin? Maxie Torlin?'

'Sure, who hasn't? Came out of Big Q about a year back.'

'That's the guy. I want to know where he is at this exact minute. Can you help me?' It was a tall order, even for a guy like Mike who knew the whereabouts of most of the big men.

'What are you, Johnny — a mind-reader or something? Torlin's been here less than twenty minutes ago.'

I sucked in a deep breath. Things were beginning to break my way after all. 'Any idea where he went, Mike?'

'Sure thing. Overheard him talking to that guy Callen. He's heading out of town. Detroit, I think. No — Chigaco. That's right. He's taking the night train. If you want him that bad, Johnny, you'll have to hurry. That train leaves in less than an hour from the depot.'

'Thanks, Mike. I'll do my best to make it.' I rang off, switched off the light and walked quickly to the window. My shadow was still there and now he had been joined by another dark shape. There was a car at the end of the street standing close to the kerb, without lights. It all looked too innocent to be anything but what it was. The big fix for Johnny Merak. They didn't intend that I should leave this place alive. They were acting under Torlin's orders all right. Keeping me there until he slipped out of Los Angeles for Chicago.

Working in total darkness, I went to the back of the apartment and checked the view from there. It looked deserted, about as empty as any place could be. Only it had that air of waiting over it that scared me a little. I knew it wasn't going to be as easy as that to get out of here, but I had to reach the rail depot before that train left for Chicago. If Maxie Torlin was on it, I wanted to be there too.

There was no time to warn Grenville or Dawn. Checking the heavy Luger, I slipped it into my pocket and went out the back way. Not a sound from the street. The low wall at the bottom of the pathway had an iron-grille gate set in it. I opened it quietly, glanced round the corner. There were a couple of lamps ten yards away, throwing a thin circle of yellow light. Outside of the circle, there was blackness and nothing that moved.

I'd taken a couple of steps along the street when the shadow detached itself from the wall. Freezing, I hugged the brickwork. He was a tall slender guy with a hatchet face. He hadn't seen me but he had only to turn his head and he would. I had to move fast and silently. Once I alerted those other guys in the next street at the front of the block, they'd be on me before I could finish this hoodlum.

He had his head half-turned as if warned by some hidden instinct when the heel of the gun caught him behind the right ear. There had been a snarl on his thin lips, almost as if he knew what was going to happen, but the expression soon gave way to one of vacancy as he pitched forward to his knees, then flopped onto his face as I hit him again. I paused onto long enough to take the gun from his pocket and pitch it over the wall, then took to my heels and ran along the narrow, deserted street as if all of the devils in hell were on my heels.

At the end of the street, I turned left,

away from the main road. Less than five minutes later, I picked up the cab cruising along the empty alleys of the city.

'You look as if you've been in one hell of a fight, buster,' said the guy behind the wheel.

'The other guy's on his way to hospital,' I said, forcing a grin.

'I can believe that. Where to, buster?'

'Central Depot and fast. There's a train leaving for Chicago around midnight and I've got to be on it.'

'O.K. Hang onto your seat.' He put his foot down on the accelerator and soon we were among the bright lights and wide streets. I leaned back, tried to rest my aching body, and watched the panorama of coloured neon lights flash by in a blur of light on both sides. Pretty soon, if not already, the unconscious body of that hoodlum would be discovered by his friends in the back alley and the hunt would be on. They might figure that I was after Torlin, that I knew where he was going, or they might not. But I was banking on the fact that the train would be out of Los Angeles and on its way before they could get around to warning Torlin.

Eleven-forty-six.

We cut through the late-night traffic, drew up outside the rail depot. I got out, gave the driver ten dollars and ran up the steps into the main booking hall.

Eleven-forty-nine.

I threw a quick, intuitive look about me. There were several people waiting for trains, but two in particular took my notice. Both were standing over by the news-stand, papers in front of their faces. They were clearly scanning the faces of everybody within range, looking for somebody in particular.

I paid some attention to them as I walked forward slowly. They were types, but from that distance, it was impossible to tell whether they were cops or Callen's hirelings, sticking around to make sure that nothing went wrong, that Johnny Merak, or the cops didn't butt in at the wrong moment and hustle Torlin off. I smiled grimly. They didn't miss a trick.

At that time of night, there was plenty of shade in the big hall and it wasn't difficult for me to slip past them and buy myself a ticket on the same train as Maxie Torlin. The clerk was apologetic, but there wasn't a sleeping berth available, but if I saw the conductor on the train, it was possible I might get a cancellation, or there might be one available somewhere along the route.

I took the ticket, picked up my change and took up my stance a little distance from the barrier, well out of sight of the watchdogs near the news-stand, but close enough to be able to spot Torlin when he arrived. The platform was empty at the moment, but I guessed that the train would steam in at any moment and that Torlin would try to push through with the crowd, just in case there were any enterprising young cops waiting for him.

Eleven-fifty-five.

Passengers began to gather in front of the barrier to the platform. A couple of minutes later, the train came steaming slowly in. I stood and waited. At least, I'd be the one guy in the world Torlin would never expect to see waiting for him. Not that I intended to show myself until I was good and ready. I disregarded the fear that cut through my mind as I spotted him in the distance, coming towards the crush of folk around the barrier with long, quick steps. There was nobody with him, but as he passed the news-stand, the two guys moved away from their positions and fell into step behind him, a discreet distance away, but close enough to move in if trouble threatened.

They passed through the barrier and onto the platform. I gave them a minute and then presented my ticket. Torlin and his two henchmen slipped into a coach at the front of the train. I picked the nearest compartment to theirs and settled down. I still hadn't thought what my next step would be, undecided whether to tail them to Chicago or try to stop them on the train. Once in Chicago, there was always the chance that I might lose them, whereas on the train, there was nowhere they could go.

Five minutes later, we moved out. The lights of the city passed us and then there was only darkness outside. We ran into November fog a few miles out and the train was forced to slow. I leaned back against my seat and felt myself shiver. But it was only partly from the cold. Those two hoodlums with Torlin represented a menace which would not be easy to get rid of. If I wanted to get Torlin to myself, I would have to deal with those two hirelings and at the depot they looked tough and efficient men who hardly ever slept and then only in relays so that there would always be one of them wide-awake.

The fog outside the window made it seem even more hopeless, but after half an hour, I got up, saw the old dame across from me throw me a funny look, then stepped over her corns into the corridor outside. I pretty soon located the berth occupied by Maxie Torlin. It wasn't difficult to spot. Because the berths on either side of it were occupied by his henchmen.

My watch said twelve-forty. I decided to tackle them one at a time and trust my luck a little further. I'd banked on both guys leaving their doors unlocked so that they could get into action quickly if there should be any trouble. My luck held. The knob twisted as I threw the door open and stepped inside, blinking in the harsh glare from the bulb set close to the roof.

The big beefy guy on the bunk had a holster strapped across his chest and the gun in it was halfway out when he froze as I covered him.

'That's better,' I said softly. I hadn't seen this guy before in my life. Probably he had been brought in from out of town to protect Torlin. Perhaps they couldn't trust the men in the mob when there might be pressure brought to bear on them from other quarters.

His face was locked into that kind of hardness which left no room in it for emotion. He looked, and was, dangerous. I leaned forward carefully, and pulled the gun from his holster while he glared up at me with hate-filled eyes.

'Who're you?' he hissed finally.

'If you don't know now, it'll be healthier for you if you never know,' I said, standing a little distance away from the door. Even though I'd taken the precaution of locking it, I still didn't want anybody charging at it and sending me sprawling into the middle of that small berth where this guy would be simply waiting to pick me off.

'Copper?' he asked thinly.

I shook my head. 'Not exactly. Just call me a free-lance dectective who sometimes works for the cops.'

Something evil flickered momentarily through his eyes. It might have been the beginning of anger, or even a smile. But if it were, it never reached his lips.

'If you're after dough or information, you've come to the wrong place.' He licked his lips. I could almost hear his brain working overtime inside his head, wheels turning within wheels as he tried to figure out why I was there. He lay quite still on one elbow, then shrugged. He probably couldn't see any connection.

'I don't get this,' he snarled finally. 'Just what are you expecting to get out of this?'

'From you, very little. I'm more interested in the big guy in the next berth.'

That surprised him. I could see that he thought nobody knew about that. Something flickered through his eyes again and

I guessed that this was the nearest he ever came to showing fear.

'I don't know what you're talking about,' he muttered stubbornly.

'Come now.' I leaned forward and deliberately exerted a little more pressure on the trigger of the gun. Sweat popped out in little beads on his forehead and he wiped the film away impatiently with the back of his hand. 'You don't want to say anything foolish, not when there's a gun on you. Believe me, I'll use this if I have to with the greatest of pleasure. And you'll have noticed by now that there's a silencer on it. Nobody will hear a sound over the noise of the train, not even your boss Maxie Torlin next door.'

His mouth was opened a trifle and stayed that way. He tried to read the answers in my face but I wasn't giving anything away either.

'I don't — '

I slammed down on the back of his wrist with the barrel of the gun, the foresight cutting a deep channel in his flesh. The blood oozed slowly from it, staining the sleeve of his immaculate white shirt. He stared down at it, lips still parted, and the pain showed through a little in his eyes, but he had not uttered a single sound.

'Don't fool around with me,' I said harshly. 'I'll make it really hurt the next time. I know that Maxie Torlin is going to Chicago and he isn't going there for his health. You're going to tell me why he's going — and where.'

'I don't know.' Some of the yellow was beginning to show through now, the fear tinging his voice. It lifted a little in pitch and he almost squealed with fright as I lifted the gun again. 'I tell you, I don't know. All I was told was to go with him to Chicago and see that he got there in one piece; that the cops were on his tail.'

'Do you know why they're looking for him?' I asked smoothly.

'Something about slaying a Judge,' he muttered sullenly. 'But what's this to you? Why are you so interested in Torlin?'

'Let's say that I don't like his face. That I intend to do something about it, shall we?'

'You're a goddamned fool if you think

you can mess with a guy like him and still remain in one piece for long.'

'I've tried it with bigger fish than him,' I said ominously, and saw from the look on his face that my words had struck home. He was no longer sure of himself, no longer sure of the fact that, if the worst came to the worst, a guy as big as Torlin could protect him. This wasn't just a rival gang matter. He knew better than that. This was something bigger. No guy in his right mind would go around threatening a big-shot like Maxie Torlin, especially to one of his own henchmen. Not unless he was pretty sure of himself.

'I think he's going to Chicago to knock off another of those people on that murder list he carries about with him. That's true, isn't it?'

His face closed up like a clam and I knew that I was right.

The train rounded a curve. I'd been wondering when this guy was going to make his pitch. It would have to come soon, that much I was sure of. It was as if the slight swerve of the cloach was the pre-determined signal he had been waiting for. I saw his feet getting ready to launch him forward, a split second before he did so.

I hadn't wanted to kill him. There were a lot of other questions he might have been able to answer. I felt sure he had been lying about not knowing where Torlin intended to go and what he meant to do once he got to Chicago; but I never got around to asking questions. The thug could have been made to talk, but not by a dear Johnny Merak.

Instinctively, I squeezed the trigger, felt the heavy weapon jerk against my wrist. The fain plop was inaudible to anybody outside the berth. There was scarcely any sound at all. Only the dark, circular hole that appeared between the hoodlum's eyes as he came clawing his way forward off the bunk, hands outstretched fingers curled in a claw-like grip, reaching for my hand.

There was nothing more to be done there. Nobody would think of looking in on the guy until the morning, unless it was Torlin or his other hired killer and I doubted whether they would talk to the conductor. They'd be too busy scouring the train trying to find the murderer.

The corridor was still empty when I stepped out, closing the door of the berth quietly behind me. The corpse on the floor looked a little pathetic and out of place so I switched off the light before I left.

There was no sound from either of the two compartments next door. I figured that the guy I had killed had been on watch and the other two were possibly asleep. I realised I was still holding the Luger in my right hand and placed it quickly in my pocket. The coach rattled and swayed and I guessed that we had passed out of the fog belt and were picking up speed, trying to make up the lost time.

I still had the other hoodlum to take care of before I could consider having a talk with Maxie Torlin. I approached the other guy's door and was on the point of turning the handle when it opened abruptly and I found myself face to face with the hoodlum. His surprise was almost as great as mine. His eyes narrowed dangerously. I cursed the fact that I had pocketed the Luger. There was no time to pull it out of my pocket now. The other guy was coming at me and fast.

I know what he would be like, that he'd be a dirty fighter when he hadn't a gun in his hand. A killer who hoped to cripple within seconds, a pair of stiffened fingers in the eyes, all of his weight behind the first, cruel punch to the belly and no holds barred.

Before he could get himself fully on balance, I had swung back, helped by the slight lurch of the train. His fist grazed over my shoulder, just catching the side of my face. I lunged forward and my head hit him full in the chest, just above the heart. It was like a hand grenade going off in that tightly confined space. As he fell back under the force of the blow, my skull came up and hit him under the chin. Normally it would have been a stunning blow, if not a knock-out one, but this guy seemed to be made of iron. He grunted then came in again, swinging his ham-like fists at my face. My bruised jaw took another swinging right and I almost screamed out aloud with the pain of it as it crunched against my jaw. We fell to the floor, his knees coming up and hitting me in the solar plexus, driving the air out of my lungs. We rolled against the side of the bunk and he brought three chopping right hands against my cheek. I could feel blood from an opened wound and it served to throw him off and get on top of him, my knees astride his chest. I hit him twice with the heel of my hand on the neck. He jerked twice, then lay still.

The fight was over. I stood up, shaking a little, and not from the jerking motion of the train. My hand rubbed my face and the side of my head. It came away with a smear of blood on the back. The thing I was happy about at that moment was that my teeth weren't spread out all over the floor of the small compartment. It would have been a teeth-knocked-out fight if it had continued. This guy had been quick off the ball and playing for keeps even though he hadn't been able to go for his gun.

I shook my head slowly to clear it, holding onto the wall for support, mental and physical. In spite of the clattering of the wheels on the rails, it was possible that Torlin had heard that rumpus and would be coming to investigate and when he did, he'd be taking no chances, possibly waiting for me once I stepped out into the corridor.

No time to take chances with Maxie Torlin now. From what I knew of him, he was more dangerous than either of these two characters. I slipped out into the corridor, expecting his door to open at any moment. I'd reached the end of the corridor before it did and I saw his figure framed in the opening. He stood for a moment glancing up and down the darkened passage, then he went inside the door to his right.

Now all hell was going to be let loose, I thought. Unless I watched myself, the tables could be turned with a vengeance here. I could be trapped, just as easily as I had set out to trap him. I felt my fingers bite into the palms of my hands. The big thing now was to get away from the scene before Torlin spotted me and started coming for me once he'd wakened the guy I'd put to sleep with the rabbit punches.

The train thundered on into the night and I had the sudden, funny feeling that either Maxie Torlin or myself could quite easily be dead, as dead as that guy in the further compartment, before we reached our destination.

8

Murder He Says

Along the corridor of the swaying train and into the next car. Get away from that area quickly, Merak, and give yourself time to think. Time to ponder on what steps to take when Maxie Torlin comes for you. I knew that if I spotted him first, I'd probably have to kill him. It was no use trying to fight off a guy like that with your fists and hope to take him alive. He would never expose himself to the danger of physical damage, he'd send in that gun-happy monkey of his to smoke me out first; and if I knew anything of that guy's nature, he'd come willingly, thirsting for blood — my blood.

He had looked as mean a character as the first guy I'd been forced to kill and once a guy like that was roughed up, he'd never forget it until his assailant was lying in a pool of his own blood. I passed through the car and moved on. Here were the main sleeping berths and everything seemed quiet. Once, one of the conductors gave me a funny look, but I kept on going, mumbling something incoherent under my breath before he could stop me. No sense in saying there was a killer on my tail. He'd have laughed in my face and turned me over to any cops who might be around as a suspected nut.

Less than a couple of minutes later, they came after me. It hadn't taken Torlin long to sober up his man and they knew by now that the other bodyguard was dead. They also seemed to have known which way I'd gone, or perhaps I'd drawn a stretch of rotten luck and they weren't sure. I spotted them from the shadows at the end of the car, working their way along, silently and methodically. They didn't seem to be leaving any stone unturned in their efforts to get Johnny Merak. And time was on their side now. They knew I couldn't get off the train unless I took my life in my hands and jumped and at the speed we were travelling now, trying to make up for the time lost in the fog, I'd break my neck for sure if I did that. In the pitch blackness outside, it would be impossible to pick a good place to fall, even if the train slowed.

I felt hemmed in. Cautiously, I worked my way along the next car and into the one behind that. I'd passed through the line of sleeping berths now and here were the ordinary compartments where those unlucky enough not to get a berth tried to sleep as best they could.

Torlin and his henchman would soon move through the cars behind me. They'd know that it was highly unlikely I'd been able to get a berth and I wouldn't risk the rumpus I'd kick up if I tried to get into one already occupied. I could sense them moving in for the kill. It wouldn't be done openly. They couldn't afford to make any fuss. I'd be taken away to some dark spot and slugged there. Then my body would be pitched out of the train into the darkness and the night would swallow me up. That way, Torlin would be sure I was finished.

Frankly, it was an idea which didn't

appeal to me. I still had the gun, but I couldn't use it when other, innocent folk might get themselves in the way of a bullet. I reached the end of the car and dived into the shadows a split second before they hit the other end.

Time was running at a high premium. No place to hide and death stalking at the back of me. There are only a few ways you can kill a guy on a place like a train. Bump him on the head in some quiet corner, use a silenced revolver and push his body through a door. There are others, but they aren't so useful or so quiet; and above everything, I knew that Torlin wanted me killed quietly.

I glanced into one of the compartments. A couple of elderly dames asleep in opposite. Three other guys reading, one with his head nodding forward on his chest. No chance there. I moved on.

I felt like a rat in a corner, a tight corner. One guy I could fight, but not two, alert and cautious and moving in for the kill. I stopped. Inside the compartment next to me, five guys playing poker, two with their backs to me, the others holding their cards glued to their bellies, eyes down. It looked the same old game as I had seen in a dozen crap houses in downtown L.A. But it was a way out for me and I took it.

Sliding open the door, I stepped inside. A lot of sets of eyes looked up suddenly, watching me, looking me over. One man, big and broad-shouldered, bald-headed, nodded affably, but his eyes were narrowed, sizing me up.

'Care to join us in a little friendly game, friend?' he asked. His voice was pleasant enough, but he was thinking quickly. Probably he had me figured as one of two types of guy. Either a real ripe cookie ready for plucking, or a sharpie trying to get in on the game and start chiselling.

'Sure,' I nodded. 'Been looking for a little action since I got on the train.'

I squeezed in between a couple of the guys, my back to the door, my hat pulled well over my eyes. It was dim inside the compartment. Whether they'd made it so deliberately or not, I couldn't tell, but it suited my purpose admirably and I didn't squawk.

'What are the stakes?' I asked.

The big guy sighed a little. I knew he was still wondering what kind of guy I was, but he didn't really care. Once the game got under way, in a little while, he'd know. Until then he'd bide his time.

'Ten dollar limit,' he said sharply. 'O.K. by you?'

'Fair enough,' I nodded. Even at ten, you could drop quite a lot in an hour.

It didn't take long to realise that it was the same old game, rigged now that a stranger was playing. They were sharping the cards whenever they got the chance and the way they worked it, it was obvious that they had been in this game for some time. I didn't bother to let on that I could see through their game. I won small sums the first couple of hands, and then began to lose steadily.

By some sixth sense, I knew the exact moment when Maxie Torlin reached the door at my back and peered into the compartment. I could sense his presence there, tight and evil, even though I couldn't see him. Whatever happened,

I told myself fiercely, I must not look round, must give no indication that I knew he was there. He'd stand there for a long while, watching, trying to be sure, waiting for me to make the first suspicious move. The hoodlum with him might not know me from the back, but Maxie knew me quite well. If he became the least bit suspicious . . .

One of the guys in front of me glanced up. I saw him looking intently through the glass partition. Then he called loudly: 'Care to join us, friends?'

There was a brief pause. I visualised Torlin shaking his head, and then I heard his voice, oddly muffled through the glass. 'Not this time, thanks. Maybe in a little while after we've attended to some unfinished business.'

A moment later, I heard their footsteps moving off along the corridor.

'Funny guy that,' said the big man. 'Seen him around someplace before. I never forget a face, but I can't place him at the moment. That other guy with him looked as though he'd just been roughed up.'

He paused and I knew he was looking closely at me, at my bruised face and swollen lip. 'Come to think of it, friend, you don't look to be in such good condition yourself.'

I looked him straight in the eye. 'What's that to you, friend?' I asked.

'Nothing.' He flickered a quick look at the rest of his pals. I knew that there was trouble coming if I stayed around too long. I played the last hand, then excused myself. I could feel their eyes boring into the back of my neck as I slid open the glass-panelled door and stepped out into the cool draught of air blowing along the empty corridor. There were a few lights showing in the distance and we seemed to be passing through one of the smaller towns. A moment later, we roared through a maze of lines, through a brightly lit station, and then on into darkness again, lit only by winking red and green lights.

Not long now before they'd worked the whole length of the train. Then they'd come back, fast, making sure a second time.

If they got to talking to those guys in the poker game, they'd know more about me than they did at the moment. I felt in bad shape as I moved along the swaying corridor, staggering a little from side to side. It had been a foolish move on my part anyway, coming after a big guy like Torlin on my own, without telling anyone where I was going. Now I was in this mess up to my neck and if I was to get out of it alive, I'd have to do some of the fastest thinking in my life. I wished that my face and chest didn't ache so. My brain felt fuzzy and little thoughts kept flashing intermittently across it, making little sense. The train hammered its way through a tunnel. At the end of the coach, I saw the shadow a split second before I reached it. That made me stop. It might have been nothing, but on the other hand —

I thought of going back, trying to find an empty compartment. Then I hesitated, moved forward on cat feet. It was the tall hatchet-faced hoodlum. He stood with his back to me, by the door, smoking. It figured. Torlin was somewhere along the train, working his way along and this guy had been left to watch in case I tried to slip back.

No way of telling how far Torlin was away. I just had to move fast and trust to luck. It was obvious this guy thought I was miles away. I moved in on him — fast. Too late, he saw my reflection in the glass in front of him and swung to meet me.

My bunched fist caught him at the side of the face, splitting his cheek as he fell back against the door. But he was quick and tough. He came back, lunging forward, all of his weight behind the pile-driver which would have killed me if it had landed properly.

I managed to ride it on my arm and threw a quick right to his stomach. He didn't have time to tense his muscles and my fist almost went through to his backbone. He doubled up with a muttered *oof* as the air whistled through his clenched teeth. His eyes turned glassy as he fell forward, heavily, against me. I pushed him up again, jerked the gun out of his pocket with a quick, instinctive movement and hit him with the flat of the butt on the side of the face. The blow left an angry red weal on his cheek and there was blood coming from his squashed nose and smashed lip. He spat blood and tried to come at me again, but that last blow had sapped most of the strength he had left.

Apart from the gasp when I had hit him in the belly, he hadn't made a single sound. Perhaps he didn't want to attract attention while his boss came onto the scene. He may even have figured that I was in on this for some other reason and didn't know a thing about Maxie, figuring that he was all alone.

His sharp face was a dirty grey and the blood was oozing down his face and dripping off his chin as I thrust him back against the door. He was still groggy, his eyes narrowed slits.

'What's all this for?' he asked, mumbling through swollen lips.

'You're going to answer a few questions. Fast,' I snarled viciously. This was no time for finesse. I had to get what I wanted out of this guy before Torlin worked his way back.

'I don't know what you're — '

'Shut up. I'll do the asking,' I said. 'And I'm in no mood for arguing now.'

He shook his head slowly and I hit him again, hard, with my right fist. His head snapped back and the glazed look came back into his eyes, blotting out for a brief moment, the gleam of pure hate which had been there before. Steadying himself, he hung onto the door, trying to keep himself on his feet.

'Maxie Torlin is heading for Chicago. Don't try to deny it, I know you're with him, acting as bodyguard. Now, don't waste my time stalling. Where is he going when he gets to Chicago and who is he going to see?'

'I don't know anything about that, I — '

I hit him again. More blood flowed down his face where his teeth had bitten into his lower lip.

He snarled like some cornered animal. 'You don't scare me so easy.' He licked his lips.

'No?' I said softly. 'Your yellowness is showing through right this minute. And if you're thinking that perhaps Torlin will come along that corridor and step in at the middle of this little talk, I'd better disillusion you. You'll be dead the minute he turns the corridor unless you tell me what I want to know.'

I took out the Luger, thrust it into his belly and tightened my pressure on the trigger. I saw him glance down, startled, saw the beads of sweat pop out onto his face, mingling with the blood. Hell glared briefly out of his slitted eyes, and he leaned back, away from the pressure of the barrel with a little jerk.

'Now. Care to talk?'

'I don't know much. I was told to act as his bodyguard. I get paid when he's delivered safe and sound.'

'Where?' I snapped.

The other swallowed thickly, threw a swift glance along the corridor, but it was still empty. One look at my face must have told him that I meant business. He was getting scared now. He must have figured that he could easily meet the same kind of fate as the other guy who'd been in on the deal and who lay dead back there in one of the berths.

'He's got a date with some guy called Finton, just off Fourth and Eleventh.'

Finton! Edward Finton. Another of the men on that list of jurors who had sent Torlin to the State Pen. It added up. I knew that the other wasn't lying this time. I opened my mouth to ask more questions, but before I could do so, the other had jerked forward, throwing me off balance. I squeezed the trigger instinctively, heard a low grunt of pain, but knew that the bullet hadn't found a vital spot. The other had been twisting and turning at the moment I fired.

He was still strong. I knew now that he had been stalling, pretending to be groggy, waiting for a moment when he could throw me off guard. I fell back into the corridor, taking my weight on my shoulders, breaking my fall as much as possible.

He came at me savagely, stamping down with his booted heel at my throat. It was one of the usual tricks of the dirty fighter and probably the one that saved me, for I had been expecting something like that from the beginning. No time to use the gun, I dropped it and grabbed at his ankle, twisting with all of my strength. His body seemed to twist around in mid-air. He let out a small scream, then hurtled back, shoulders striking the door with a heavy thump. There was a sharp click, a sudden draught of icy air that blew about me and a thin scream that faded away into the roar of the train wheels.

Scooping up the fallen gun, I got to my feet, struggled with the door for a long moment before I managed to get it closed again. I was shaking all over as I tried to pull myself together. This was the third beating I had taken in less than twelve hours and it was beginning to tell on me. A guy couldn't go on being beaten up, without any proper sleep, and still feel in top form.

Now there was only Torlin to take care of. He was somewhere on the train. But now I felt a little better. I could either get him there, or wait until we got to Chicago now that I knew his destination. There was a rush of thoughts piling up in my mind, but I had little time in which to think them all out. The minutes and the seconds were ticking away. Maybe I had been a fool in going it all alone. Maybe I should have pulled in Grenville on the deal. But it was too late now for recriminations.

I decided to leave Torlin until we hit Chicago, unless he came looking for me in person before then. Somehow, I didn't think he would. Now that his two bodyguards were gone, he'd think twice about coming after me. So long as he had them around to take care of any big trouble, he felt safe and secure. But with them gone, he'd be a nervous guy, sitting on his nerves, wondering if and when I intended to strike again.

He couldn't afford to take any chances now. Not until he got to Chicago when he could pick up a few more hoodlums ready and willing to do his dirty work for him so long as the price was right. On the train, he was all alone now. He wouldn't be so anxious to come looking for me so long as he knew I had a gun.

Chicago looked grey and dismal and downbeat when we finally steamed in. I'd had little real sleep on the journey, keeping one eye open for trouble. But none had come. It seemed they hadn't found the body of the dead hoodlum in the berth, or if they had there had been no fuss made about it, although the cops might have been notified at Chicago and would be waiting for us at the depot.

I got out onto the platform, shivered a little in the raw wind which blew through my coat into my bones. Most of the other passengers were beginning to alight. I couldn't see Maxie, but I knew he'd be somewhere around, his scheming brain trying to turn the situation once more to his way of working. I wondered whether he'd risk showing himself if he knew I was anywhere around on the platform.

Then I spotted him. A furtive guy now that he had been stripped of his protection. In the old days, he might have been able to handle a guy like Johnny Merak by himself, with no outside help, but not now. Now he had softened up a good deal. He needed musclemen, trigger-happy gunmen to shadow him and until he met up with some more he could trust, he was no more than a rat in a box, seeking and scheming for some way of escape.

I waited at the barrier. The mass of passengers moved through and the platform began to clear. There were still a few late guys walking slowly towards the barrier, but I couldn't spot Torlin among them. Then I saw him. He stepped cautiously off the coach near the rear and began walking slowly along the draughty platform.

Even from where I stood, I could see his gaze flicking from side to side, looking for trouble, expecting it to pop out at any moment and hustle him off. He seemed wary, a little afraid, and in spite of my aches and pains, I felt good watching him that way.

Ten yards away, he suddenly looked up and saw me. The look in his eyes was one of surprise rather than fear. Then he looked away again and it was done deliberately. He knew now where the trouble lay, and he was still trying to figure out how I had managed to locate him.

He came through the barrier. I saw him watching me furtively as he moved forward. Possibly in the last few moments, he had had second thoughts about me. His face was hard. He was puzzled. My being there was something he hadn't expected, something he didn't quite understand. It was something he had to figure out — and quickly. It did something to me inside to see that first, faint touch of cringing fear on his face as I walked towards him. He would probably never understand how much I hated his guts — or why.

'Maxie,' I said softly. 'Fancy meeting you here.'

He grinned, but it was a forced smile and only just touched his lips, curling them slightly at the corners.

'Johnny. What brings you to Chicago? The last I heard of you, you were back in Los Angeles.'

'Sure, Maxie. And now I'm here and I think it's time you and I had a little heart-to-heart talk. There are a lot of things I've been trying to figure out and you seem to be in the middle of them all.'

'O.K. Johnny. If you like. Where'll I meet you?'

'No need to run out on a pal like that, Maxie,' I went on smoothly. 'We can talk quite well over a drink. I wouldn't like to lose you now, just after finding you.'

He hesitated. I could see that he wasn't quite sure of my motives. He knew I wouldn't kill him there in full view of perhaps a couple of hundred citizens. I'd wait until I got him well away from the crowds in some quiet, secluded spot. I caught his arm, propelled him out of the Station and into the street outside.

There was a red, watery sun trying to force its way through the clinging grey mist, and having plenty of trouble. No warmth in the air and I shivered again.

'By the way, Maxie,' I said as I hailed a cab. 'I'm really sorry about those two boys of yours back on the train. But they wouldn't allow me in to see you and as I've said it is important. If they'd only seen sense, they might still have been alive.'

'I was wondering about that.' Torlin's voice was suddenly hard and wary. 'I figured it might be you, Johnny. You're the only guy I know who could have pulled a job like that and get away with it. I ought to have known I suppose and killed you back there on the train. Tell me, though, how did you manage to find me?'

He was stalling for time. I couldn't see why unless he'd already made arrangements to meet somebody here and was waiting for them to turn up. I hustled him inside the cab as it drew up at the kerb and slipped in beside him.

'Where to, bud?'

'Just drive around for a little while,' I said quickly. 'My friend and I have some important business to discuss.'

'O.K. bud. So long as you've got the fare.'

We pulled away from the kerb. I breathed a little easier. Still no sign of trouble. I guessed that Maxie Torlin was doing some of the fastest thinking in his life, at that moment.

'Now,' I turned to Torlin, 'let's get down to facts before I have to finish you permanently.'

'You'll never get away with it, Merak. Not here, in Chicago. Remember, this used to be my home territory. They haven't forgotten me here. Once I've finished what I've set out to do, I'll come back again. But that can wait.'

'So you think you're going to kill every man and woman on that jurors list.'

'You going to try to stop me?' There was a little too much confidence in his voice. I didn't like it. But so far, I couldn't figure on where he got it from. I threw a swift glance in the driver's mirror, but could see nothing following us. He might have a couple of cars cruising at a discreet distance behind us, but if he had, then they were still some distance away. Not close enough to cause any immediate trouble.

I didn't say anything, I just waited for him to do the talking. That way, he might tell me a lot more than if I'd asked direct questions.

'I've got men tailing us right now, Merak. You can kill me, perhaps, but you'd be dead within minutes of it. Is it worth it, just for some hatred you've got of me. It can't be anything more than that. I've had nothing to do with you in the past, so it can't be any grievance from the old days. Just what is it that's eating you?'

Smooth words, an oily tongue, trying to make me lower my guard for that fraction of a second which would be all he'd need to turn things to his own advantage.

'Shall we say I don't like your face?' I said thinly. 'And I don't like the way you carry on this personal vendetta against decent, ordinary men and women who only did their job on that day five years ago when you went to the Pen.'

'They sent me there,' exploded the other fiercely. I felt shocked by the depth of his anger. There was a faint touch of insanity to his voice, and I felt a shiver go through me even though I held the whiphand at the moment. 'I swore I'd pay them all back, in full. And that's what I'm doing. But what's all this to you? You used to be like that in the old days. Is it possible you could have changed so much in five years?'

'I've changed,' I said harshly. 'And for

the better. I feel a hell of a lot cleaner than I did then. But you wouldn't understand that. You're a dirty, rotten crook, bad to the core. You'll never change.'

He smiled thinly, even at the insults. I settled back in my seat. All hell was set to break loose at any minute and here we were, the two central figures in the play, talking together in the back of a cab as if we were long-lost brothers.

'I reckon you must be insane if you think you can get away with killing thirteen men and women. And you always want to shoot them up yourself. You couldn't send out a couple of your boys to do the dirty jobs for you. Oh no, you have to see your victims squirm before you put a few bullets into them. What kind of a kick do you get out of that, Torin?'

'You've never seen the inside of San Quentin,' he muttered harshly. He turned his head away for a minute, staring out through the window at the sidewalks drifting greyly past. There was more bitterness than madness in his voice now.

I could guess how he felt in a way. For a big man such as he had been in his hey day, it must have been galling to be sent to Big Q for six years on a double-cross. All the time, for him, there would have been trouble, but he had been big enough to handle it his way. Rival syndicates and people with bright ideas. Men who couldn't be trusted. Yet, for long enough, he had survived. Then had come the crash. In the end, because of a double-cross, he had been fixed so good that not even his smart lawyer had managed to get him off the hook.

That must have hurt. All of those long years in that grey house, thinking over what had happened, brooding over it, planning his revenge. Now he was out and that revenge had begun. A cold-blooded killer. I knew he'd stop at nothing to complete his self-imposed mission of destruction.

I had to stop him. Leaning forward, not taking my eyes off Torlin for a single minute, I rapped sharply on the glass window of the cab.

The driver half-turned his head. I knew

that Torlin was watching me curiously out of the corner of his eye, wondering what I was going to do.

'Take us to Police Headquarters,' I said tightly. 'Hurry!'

'Yes, sir.' The driver stepped on the gas and we moved quickly, threading our way through the thickening traffic.

Torlin said thinly, 'That wasn't a wise thing to do, Merak. As you'll soon find out.'

'The time for wisdom was past a long time ago when it came to killers like you,' I said hoarsely. 'Once I've handed you over to the authorities and know that you're safely behind bars, I'll feel a little easier in my mind. I reckon I can get plenty of evidence this time that'll stick. And it'll be a murder rap you'll be facing now, not just a six-year sentence. It'll be the chair for you, the end of the road.'

His lips curled into a sneering grin. 'Pretty soon, you'll overstep yourself, Merak.'

I shook my head. 'Somehow, I doubt whether you've got the police in your pocket now, Torlin. If you have, there's a guy back in Los Angeles who'll be only too pleased to take care of you.'

The cab moved in to the kerb, slowed. I got out first, keeping the gun under the sleeve of my coat, but trained on Torlin all of the time. He got out slowly. I wondered when he would make his play. It would have to be soon — but I felt ready for it.

'Here you are, bud,' said the driver. If he noticed anything out of the ordinary, he gave no outward sign. 'The local precinct is down that street there, right at the bottom.'

He pointed. The narrow street cut through between a couple of blocks of buildings and I could just make out the station at the far end. I nodded, handed him a ten-spot, then motioned Maxie along ahead of me.

I stared in front of me over Torlin's shoulder. I didn't see anything — just dirty bricks, soggy cigarette stubs in the gutter and pieces of dirty paper which had been ground underfoot.

I heard the faint scraping sound at the back of me, like feet moving over the bricks. I turned sharply, instinctively, but not fast enough. Something thudded against the side of my head and the ground slanted up and hit me in the face. The gun dropped with a faint clatter from my nerveless fingers. I wriggled onto my side and tried to get up.

There was a muttered curse from somewhere over my aching head and a foot slammed twice against my ribs making me want to scream with the pain. Out of the corner of my blurred vision, I saw a hand reach down and pick up my gun from where it had fallen.

Gasping for breath, I tried to roll away towards the wall, but somebody jumped onto my back, stood there, their weight driving all of the air out of my lungs. It was all I could do to keep the air going down into my chest. My teeth bit into the gutter and I couldn't move.

A voice said out of the dimness, 'I warned you, Merak, if you kept riding me that you'd find yourself in trouble. But you wouldn't listen.' Maxie Torlin's voice. I shivered.

The feet stepped off my back and I could breathe a little easier. I sucked air down into my lungs, heard it rasping in my throat. But the respite didn't last for long.

Somebody else moved up out of the shadows which seemed to be pressing in on me from all sides, ringing me round. I couldn't make out any more than the bare outline of the man, but when he spoke, I knew why I'd fallen for this sucker trick, why Torlin had been so supremely confident in the cab.

'You always were an impulsive fool, Merak. It's a pity you went over to the other side. I could have used a man like you in my organisation.' That had been Harry Callen's voice. He was here in Chicago. The big guns were moving in together.

I tried to say something, but the words wouldn't come and it hurt whenever I moved the muscles of my throat. I wanted to roll over so that I could see them, glare up at them defiantly. But my body seemed paralysed. There was anger in my bruised mind, but little fear. Anger at allowing myself to fall for such a fool trick.

It was even possible that Callen had deliberately allowed the news of Torlin's departure to drop so that somebody would pick it up and report back to me. Now they had lured me away from any help I might have expected in Los Angeles. I was out on a limb here and unless I misjudged these hoodlums, it wasn't intended that I should remain a menace to them for much longer. There would be a quick ride, and an even quicker death at the end of it; and this time, they would make no mistakes.

'Get him out of here,' said Callen's voice. 'There isn't much time. The car's at the end of the alley.'

I struggled to get to my knees, but something hit me soggily behind the ear. A million coloured lights exploded inside my brain and this time, I went all the way out. In a way I felt glad. It was a lot like falling asleep and there was no pain . . .

9

The End of Death

The dried blood was still there encrusting my cheek. I tried to sit up, but it was impossible to move and everything seemed to be tilting and whirling in a slow circle, with myself as the central axis. I shut my eyes and opened them again. My body ached terribly and I had the feeling that my ribs were sticking out through my jacket.

'He's coming round,' said a voice, drifting in from nowhere.

'Good.' Another voice that sounded like gravel being mixed. 'I always reckon it's best when they know what's going to happen to them before they go.'

A man moved into my line of vision, blurred by the nauseous ache at the back of my temples. I squinted up at him. The undulating motion continued and I couldn't quite figure it out. Beneath me there was something hard, but curved at the sides so that I couldn't stretch myself out straight, but had my legs tucked underneath me, my arms tied with thick rope.

'So you're Johnny Merak,' said the first voice. 'I heard about you from way back. Used to be one of the top men in the L.A. Organisation some four or five years back. I wonder what turned you sour so suddenly.'

I stared at him out of dazed eyes. Gradually, the details focused. He looked tough and efficient. The man beside him, looking down at me out of pale, empty eyes, was the real killer type. The kind of guy who'd drop his own mother for a lousy hundred bucks. I squeezed my eyes shut and tried to concentrate. Several seconds fled before I realised that the undulating motion of my surroundings was real and not illusory. One of the men came over, gripped me by the shoulders and pulled me upright.

'Better take a good look at your surroundings while you've got the chance, sucker,' he said harshly.

I saw what I had begun to suspect. There was water all around us. Grey, dirty water reaching away into the fog which shrouded us almost completely. It was impossible to say how far we were from land. I couldn't see that far and there was no way of telling how long I had been unconscious. All that was certain, was that I was intended for a watery grave. Pretty soon, unless a miracle happened, I'd be feeding the fishes.

'You're being foolish if you think you'll get away with murder like this,' I said stiffly.

The big guy laughed as though it was the biggest joke of the year.

'Yeah. You ain't going nowhere, pal. And Maxie reckons you're all alone. There's nobody knows you're even in Chicago.'

'That's where you're wrong,' I said, trying to force conviction into my voice. 'Do you think I'd be stupid enough to come here without letting anybody know where I was? They'll connect you with Big Maxie all right. Don't worry about that.'

'Shut up!' snarled the thin-faced guy. He slammed me hard across the face with the side of his stiffened hand. I fell back against the side of the boat, unable to help myself, my arms strapped tightly.

'Maxie does the talking, not you,' he growled. The other guy brought up a gun and said some uncomplimentary things about me under his breath.

'And you're the guy who does the shooting.'

I got another lesson from the gun for my pains. The dull splash of the water against the side of the boat was beginning to get on my nerves. The grating laughter of the big gorilla at the front of the boat lowered my blood temperature to the level of the sea outside.

'Here?' muttered the thin-faced guy. He turned to the other, standing in the bows. 'We ought to be far enough away from the shore now. Besides, I've never known a guy yet who could swim back with his hands tied behind his back.' He laughed again and the little shivers worked overtime as they ran up and down my spine.

The fog had closed in upon us now. It was impossible to see more than five yards in any direction. I saw the big gorilla coming towards me as I lay trussed like a chicken. No time to pray now. No time to do anything, even if I was in a position to do anything. This is the end of Johnny Merak, smart guy, fall guy for the big-time crooks, I thought. No chance of getting out of this deal.

'This is what I've been waiting for,' grated the big guy as he stood over me, straddling me with his legs. His face leered down at me, uneven, nicotine-stained teeth showing through his parted lips. 'Just to watch a guy like you squirm. You've only got a few minutes to live, Merak. Any last requests?'

'Stop the talking and get on with it,' snarled the other guy. 'I'm catching my death of pneumonia here waiting for you to get rid of this wise guy.'

'Haw, haw,' rasped the gorilla. He bent and grasped the ropes around my hands and waist, meaning to heave me into the water. What happened next was kinda hazy. Something huge and massive loomed up out of the grey fog, something knife-shaped that rose more than twenty-five feet above us. The sea was no longer a sullen, smooth thing that slapped quietly against the boat. It rose up in a vast, creaming bow wave, bearing down upon us, smashing against the side of the boat.

There was a moment of madness. The thin-faced guy screamed something thinly at the bow of the boat, a shout that was drowned instantly in the roaring wave as the bow of the vessel crunched into the side of the boat, smashing it like matchwood. The thin guy threw up his arms and vanished in an instant as the metal took him full in the chest, shearing sideways over the boat. The beefy guy took no further interest in me. I saw him pitch forward into the turbulent water. The next minute, I went in myself, down into a bubbling froth of water that rushed in my ears and stopped my mouth, shutting off the scream that formed in my throat.

This was indeed the end. Whether I got tossed into the water by that huge gorilla or by the bow of a steamer cutting into the boat, it was all the same in the end. I came to the surface, struggling insanely to free myself of the ropes that tied my hands and arms together behind my back. But the water had shrunk them still further and all I got was a pair of cut wrists for my pains. I went down again. Everything was a confused riot of sound that made no sense. My whole past flashed in front of me. I'd often heard that — this was the first time I had experienced it for myself and it was one hell of a feeling.

There was the thunder of the water in my ears as I came up, spluttering and gasping for the second time. No time to wonder what had happened to the two thugs who had brought me out here to drown me. If they hadn't been drowned themselves by now, they would be threshing about there in the water somewhere, possibly yelling their fool heads off, only I doubted whether anybody would hear them or see them.

In that brief, flashing second, when I could almost hear the gentleman with the scythe whispering my name in my ear, the people and events of the past week moved in front of my eyes like a ghostly parade and I couldn't shut them out. People and places appeared in precise order. Harry Callen and my meeting with Maxie Torlin. The flight from Callen's country house, the scene in Grenville's office when we had finally tracked down the identity of the slayer. The train journey and my own fool mistakes at the end of it when it seemed that I had everything wrapped up neatly and in my pocket. Johnny Merak, the fool hero.

It was like watching some strange movie in a dream. Only this time, there wasn't going to be any awakening at the end of it — only death. The water rose up in front of my stultified vision. My throat and mouth were choked with it. I opened my mouth to yell something and then there was only darkness again.

* * *

Very slowly, I climbed up the dark steps towards consciousness. Voices were sounding a long way off and I couldn't make sense out of the jumbled words. Something caught at me and rolled me over onto my stomach and I felt so weak and tired that I couldn't protest. I thought it had to be that big gorilla, getting ready to pick me up bodily and toss me into that black, swirling water.

I coughed and something dribbled out of the corner of my mouth. It felt like blood, only there was a sharply stinging taste like salt on my lips and my throat felt caked and dry. I tried to swallow but the action hurt my throat. My lips and tongue burned as though I had drunk acid and it seemed as though a red-hot wire had been thrust down my throat into my stomach, right down into my body, tickling my heels from the inside.

I struggled to get to my knees, but something heavy and firm held me down. Everything swam in a whirling haze in front of my eyes, but I knew that there was light there, an intense, blinding light and the voices had started up again.

Was this what it was like to be dead? I wondered vaguely. It wasn't like anything I had ever imagined. I realised that I was clutching something in my right hand and I held my fingers close up against my eyes. A voice, very close to my ear said:

'Looks as though he's coming round now, Doc. Think he'll be O.K.?'

'Should be.' The voices came and went like fragments of a nightmare. My legs doubled up and I vomited. After that, I felt a little better. My vision cleared and the room stopped swinging around me.

I mumbled something and a dark figure seemed to detach itself from the haze and move forward. There was the touch of cool fingers on my forehead where it burned like fire. The figure knelt beside me and held a bottle to my lips. I swallowed gratefully, felt liquid trickle down my throat in a cooling, soothing stream. It tasted wonderful, whatever it was, but I couldn't keep that first mouthful down. The second time I tried, gulping at it like an insane man dying of thirst, it stayed down and the other, after withdrawing the bottle, felt at my wrist for my pulse.

'What — ' I gasped.

'Lie still and don't try to talk just now,'

said a quiet voice. 'We'll soon have you on your feet again.'

The lean face was grim as it bent over me, the eyes watching me shrewdly from behind steel-rimmed glasses. He seemed to be counting to himself, finally nodding.

'Not too bad. A little slow and irregular, but you'll soon be O.K. You've had a pretty bad time of it. Lucky we pulled you out of the water when we did, fellow.'

Little thoughts began to come back to me. My memory seemed to be returning in fragments as if my brain was having trouble in collecting everything which had happened in the past. Then I remembered being in that boat with those two hoodlums whose orders had been to toss me overboard as soon as we were far enough from the shore, with a weight around my neck so that my body wouldn't be washed up in the near future and no embarrassing questions would be asked.

'What happened to the other two guys?' I managed to get the words out in a tumbling rush.

The other shook his head gravely. 'I'm afraid you were the only one we found.'

'It doesn't really matter. They deserved everything they got.'

'Why talk like that about the dead?' he asked gently.

I tried to smile but failed miserably. 'You didn't know them, doc. You couldn't feel any human thoughts towards guys like that. I suppose you've guessed by now what was happening?'

'Some of it. It wasn't difficult to put two and two together and arrive at some kind of answer, even if it wasn't quite four.'

'They had me out there to murder me, to bump me off if you like.'

'Why?'

'That's a leading question, doc. But I'll answer it if you're interested. My name's Johnny Marek. I'm a private investigator. There've been three murders in Los Angeles over the past week, all committed by one man. A big-shot named Max Torlin. He got out of San Quentin almost a year ago. Since then, he's been systematically murdering the Judge and

214

members of the jury who sent him up for a six-year stretch, five years ago. He's already killed the first two members of the jury and Judge Buchanan. I trailed him to Chicago where he's due to kill another guy called Frinton. If I can't get to this man first, he's as good as dead right now.'

The other nodded slowly. 'You're in no fit condition to do anything about it, Mister Merak,' he said gravely. 'You've just been rescued from drowning. I reckon you've been as near to death without actually dying as any man I've known.'

'But don't you see, doc. I'm the only one who can save this guy Frinton. He's in deadly danger.'

'O.K. O.K.' The other sighed. 'But lie there and rest until we dock. It'll be another fifteen minutes or so before we get into port. By rights, we ought to make a report and hand you over to the authorities. If what you say is true and those men were trying to kill you, then that's something they ought to know about. They'll want to question you.'

'For God's sake, doc, there isn't time for that. Can't you get it into your head that this is a matter of life and death?'

'I see that all right.' He rose to his feet. 'I'll have a word with the Captain. I think we might be able to fix it so that you get ashore right away once we berth. You see, I saw that rope tied around your arms and wrists when they pulled you out of the water. Nobody goes into the water in that condition of his own free will.'

'Thanks, doc. I only hope I'm in time.'

I sat up and the other helped me to my feet. I leaned on the edge of the bunk and waited for the room to stop going round and round. My lips and tongue still felt hot and parched, but the milk which the other had forced down me, had soothed them and the burning let up a little as I stood there.

'Here.' The other held out a flask to me. 'This might put some of the warmth back into your bones. Take it, but sip it slowly. Call it my own personal prescription, if you like.'

I sipped it and took it easy as he left the small cabin, closing the door behind him.

The whiskey burned the back of my throat like a stream of molten iron, but it brought some of the warmth and life back into my shivering body and I could think clearly once more.

The doc came back a few minutes later with another tall, grim-faced guy behind him. From his uniform, I guessed he was the Captain. He looked at me sternly, almost as if I were a small boy he'd caught stealing apples.

'The doctor tells me that you can save a man's life if we let you off as soon as we dock, Mister Merak.' He spoke as if he wasn't sure whether to believe that or not.

'That's right, Captain,' I said wearily. 'There isn't time to give you the full story, but the guy who's trying to kill him is a maniac. He's been nursing his hatred and thirsting for revenge for the past five years while he's been in the State Penitentiary at San Quentin.'

'Very well, I'll see what I can do. It oughtn't to be too difficult.' He lifted his square shoulders. 'I'm only doing this on the doctor's recommendation. He doesn't usually make a mistake when it comes to judging a man's character. Besides — ' he grinned, ' — I noticed those ropes too.' He went out, leaving me with the doctor.

'We'll be docking in a few minutes,' said the other conversationally. 'Do you have a gun?'

I shook my head. 'They wouldn't leave that with me,' I said.

'No, of course not. How stupid of me.'

'Why, doc. Do you have one?'

'Well . . . Yes, I do happen to have one. But it's pretty old. I'm not sure whether it still works or not.'

'Let me see it.' I spoke eagerly. This was more than I had ever expected.

He rummaged around in a locker, finally came up with an old Colt pistol. It looked ancient, but it still worked with a buttered smoothness.

'Do you have any ammunition for this gun?'

'Ammunition. Oh sure, somewhere around.' He sighed, but got it for me. Twenty rounds. It was enough for what I had to do. I loaded the pistol, slipping a clip into it and working the mechanism expertly.

Ten minutes later, there was a sudden lurch and I guessed that we had docked. I stood up and moved a little unsteadily towards the door of the cabin.

'I only hope you know what you're doing,' said the other dubiously. 'Maybe you'd better contact the police on your way.'

'To hell with that,' I said, and I placed my hand on the knob of the door.

'Wait,' said the other sharply.

I turned, looked at him.

'Look,' he said in his quiet, grave voice. 'You're playing with dynamite if these people are as you say they are. Don't you think you ought to let the police handle this? You're in no fit condition to go running around Chicago. You know that they aren't fooling. If they can get you once, they can do it again. And the next time, somebody might not just happen along as we did to get you out of a watery grave.' He gave me a crooked grin.

'Thanks for the gun,' I said slowly. I dropped it into my pocket. 'If you want to call the cops to ease your own conscience, by all means do so. Tell them I'm meeting this guy Finton just off Fourth and Eleventh.'

'Somehow, I think I'll do that,' he said wearily. There was concern on his face as I stepped out in the narrow corridor, then went up on deck. The fog was still there, clinging in long grey tendrils to everything. There were a few passengers on the ship and they gave me cursory glances as I brushed past them, out onto the quayside.

Seconds later, I was in the street and heading swiftly into the main part of town. There was only one thought pounding through my tired brain now. To get to Finton before Torlin took it into his head to pay him a social visit.

It was another ten minutes before I could find a cab. 'Eleventh and Fourth,' I said sharply. 'And hurry.'

'What is this bud, a convention?'

'It could mean the difference between life and death,' I said thinly, and I meant every word I said. The other seemed to sense some of the urgency for he put his foot down on the accelerator and asked no more questions.

I shivered as I leaned back and tried to think things out carefully for the first time since I had been picked up out of the water. My clothes were still damp and hung on me in shapeless folds, but at least the hoodlums hadn't bothered to take my wallet when they had searched me for my gun. Inwardly, in spite of the aches and pains, I felt cold and calm and sick at heart. Too much time had been wasted through my own stupidity. Even though Torlin would feel pretty certain that I was finally out of the way, I didn't think he would wait long before paying his threatened call on Finton and carrying out his threat.

Impatience rode me as we were forced to slow in the middle of town. I fretted and fumed as I sat there, feeling the assuring bulge and weight of the ancient Colt in my pocket. That was another thing they wouldn't be expecting once I turned up — that I would be armed.

The cab seemed to crawl for the last half mile or so. When we finally arrived, there was nothing but the fog and a few citizens braving the chill November weather of late afternoon. I slipped the guy another ten-spot, waited until he had pulled away into the mist, then moved slowly along Eleventh Avenue, looking for the address of this guy, Finton.

Like the others, it was set a little off the main thoroughfare in a dingy back court which overlooked the backs of the flats on the opposite side. There was a droopy-faced guy sitting behind the desk and it was obvious that the place had seen far better times, but that had been a long while earlier. Now it was a backwash, a place for forgotten men and women who eked out their lives in shadow.

'Is there a guy called Finton living here?' I asked.

The man behind the desk looked at me curiously, then nodded. 'Sure. Who wants him?'

'The name's Merak, but he wouldn't know that. No sense in paging him. I'll go up and surprise him if you'll give me the number of his room.'

'You a friend of his?'

'In a way. He'll probably be pleased to see me.'

'O.K. bud. He doesn't usually have many visitors. Stays in his room most of the time. Funny guy.'

'Yeah, I'm sure he is.'

'Room twenty-seven. Up the stairs and on your right at the top.'

'O.K. I'll find it.' I walked quickly towards the stairs, paused at the bottom. Turning, I called loudly. 'Anybody else been asking for him today?'

The other shook his head lazily. 'Not while I've been here. Past five hours. I go off in a couple of hours time. Can't say about earlier this morning.'

I breathed a little easier. Quickly, I made my way up the stairs, covered with a threadbare red carpet, with most of the design worn away.

Just the kind of place I had expected. The place where a man could hope to hide away from death, once he knew that it was coming for him. At least, I figured, if nobody had been there during the past five hours, there was a good chance that I might find him still alive. I checked the gun in my pocket, eased off the safety catch just in case, determined not to be caught unawares this time. If I'd started out this case with nine lives, there could be very few of them left by now and I couldn't afford to slip up once more.

At the top of the stairs, I walked along the narrow, dusty corridor which stretched away in both directions, glancing at the numbers on the doors. The paintwork here was faded and in places the paper hung off the walls. There were cracks in the plaster of the ceiling, running like a tracery of fine pencil marks over the plaster.

A lonely guy, I thought, as I neared the end of the passage. Some guy hiding in a terrible fear, probably knowing what had happened to Judge Buchanan and two of his companions on that jury, not sure when his turn would come, but trying desperately hard to escape the fate of the others. He might even be armed, I told myself, and in that case, it was possible he wouldn't open the door to me if I knocked. He'd be ready for any trap that Torlin might try to spring on him and that, in itself, could make him a dangerous man.

Twenty-seven. It was written in faded numerals over the top of the door. I stood hesitant for a minute. No sound came from the room beyond. Maybe he was lying in there on the bed, smoking cigarette after cigarette, wondering when the call would come. There might even be a gun lying beside him, already cocked for instant use. The further Torlin worked his way down the list, the more difficult it was going to be for him to take his intended victims by surprise; and that could spell trouble for Johnny Merak. I could quite easily get a bullet through my fool brain if I went barging in there.

I knocked softly.

Still no word, no sound from inside.

'Mister Finton.' I called quietly. For a moment, I thought I heard a faint movement just inside the door, as if somebody had eased their way up to it and was standing right at the other side, breathing very softly.

'Finton?'

Still no answer. I shrugged. Reaching down I twisted the handle of the door. It was locked from the inside.

'Are you all right in there, Finton?' I was shouting hoarsely by this time. Vaguely, I was aware of the doors along the corridor opening one after the other and of the occupants stepping out into the corridor, peering inquisitively in my direction. Their eyes watched me with a sort of animal-like lack of curiosity, as if this was an everyday affair somewhere in the place.

I turned to the nearest guy, a fat man with a face that had collapsed over the years into a mess of drooping flesh. His oyster eyes were almost sunk in the flesh that surrounded them.

'Have you seen anything of Mister Finton today?' I asked.

'You from the police?'

I shook my head impatiently. 'I'm a friend of his. This could be important. Have you seen him?'

'Not since last night. He's a queer cuss. Never has a word for anybody. If you ask me, he's plain scared of something.'

The guy from the desk downstairs came hurrying up. He strutted forward, looked at me tightly.

'What's going on here?' he demanded.

'The door's locked and there's no answer from inside.' I said as quietly as I could. 'I think there's something wrong in there. Do you have a pass key?'

'I do. But there may be another explanation for why he doesn't answer. He may not be there. After all, he does go out sometimes, you know.'

'Perhaps. But I don't think so this time. Can you open this door or not?'

My tone must have scared him a little for he nodded like a frightened rabbit, produced the pass key and fitted it into the lock.

I pushed open the door, brushed past him, and stepped inside, the gun in my fist, giving the place the once-over with a single glance. At first sight, the place looked empty. I was beginning to figure that maybe the other had been right all the time, that I had made a fool of myself once more and this guy, Finton, was out taking the air in spite of the kind of day it was outside.

Then I went into the other room, at the back, and I knew that I hadn't been wrong. Maybe Finton had been scared of something, afraid to show his face as the fat man had said. But he wasn't scared of anything any longer. He'd never be scared again.

I heard the fat man's sharp intake of breath somewhere behind me as he peered over my shoulder and saw the body of the small, thin guy lying face-downwards on the floor, an ominous red stain on the threadbare carpet at the side of the bed. His arms were flung out in front of him, his legs twisted into an odd angle.

I walked forward and turned him over, looking into the fear-filled face, set in rigor. Somewhere behind me a woman screamed shrilly, a lost sound that seemed to echo and re-echo in that small room. Then there was movement at my back and the guy from behind the desk walked forward and stared down at the guy on the floor.

'This is Finton, I suppose.' I said quietly, even though I knew beforehand what the answer was going to be.

'Yes, that's Mister Finton,' said the

other in a strangled tone. 'Is he dead?'

'With half a dozen bullets in his chest, he's dead all right.' I said with a faint touch of ironic sarcasm. I got to my feet. Once again, I had been too late. The little guy had hidden himself away, but the organisation had caught up with him. The miracle at the moment was that Johnny Merak was still alive.

There was movement outside on the stairs, the sound of heavy footsteps coming along the corridor. A moment later, three cops burst into the room and advanced upon me.

'You Johnny Merak?' demanded the first one.

I nodded. 'That's right. What are you, mind-readers?'

'Not exactly. The doctor on that ship which just docked told us we'd probably find you here. Said something about trying to stop a murder.'

'I didn't make it in time, I'm afraid,' I told him. 'The poor devil was dead by the time I got here. They certainly didn't waste any time.'

The other said nothing, but took the

heavy Colt from my hand, sniffed it experimentally, then gave it back to me. I was glad I hadn't needed to fire the gun since the doctor had loaned it to me.

'Shot from a close range. At least five, possibly six bullets in his chest,' said the taller of the other two cops, straightening his back. He looked grim and efficient. 'With a chest-full of slugs like that, I reckon one at least must have got him through the heart. He must have died instantly.'

The other said nothing, but bent and examined the dead guy himself, then he got slowly to his feet, nodding. 'Been dead for some little time too.' He turned to me. 'I think you'd better come along to the Station with us Mister Merak. There are quite a lot of questions the Lieutenant will want to ask. You seem to know more about this slaying than anybody else.'

'Except for the killer,' I said thinly, as I walked towards the door.

10

The Long Ride

They were taking the empty shell of
Sam Finton away as I followed the two
cops along the corridor, down the
stairs, and out into the waiting car.
Stupid, crazy, the whole thing. I felt
empty and strange inside. What chance
was there of fighting these men? They
were in charge of so vast an
organisation that you couldn't hope to
stop them. Like some gigantic, crushing
steamroller, they would plough right
over you, brushing aside any feeble
resistance such as that put up by
Johnny Merak.

Why don't you level with yourself, I
thought savagely, and give up this crazy
idea of trying to stop Torlin. He's far
bigger than you are. He knows your every
move. Even these cops might be in his
pay, or in Callen's, reporting back to

them that you have escaped their clutches and are still on the loose, potentially dangerous, but not vitally so.

I got into the car beside the driver, while the other cop climbing into the back, crushed into the rear seat. We moved off with a wailing blare of the sirens. A crowd had a already gathered outside the dingy tenements. The mortuary wagon was there, standing a little distance away, ready to receive the body of gangsterdom's latest victim.

Through the rear window, as I twisted my head, I saw the two guys carrying the stretcher covered with a white sheet and load it into the back of the wagon. Then, and only then did I know why I would go on fighting while there was still breath left in my body, why I would never be able to give up. If I didn't then more men and women like poor, frightened Sam Finton would be shot down in cold blood, simply because they had done their duty, and sent a criminal to prison.

I shivered. It was still going to be a long and weary road I would have to travel before the score was finally settled, before this thing was finished, one way or another, for both Callen and Torlin. Not until they were both safely out of the way, would I be able to relax and feel like a human being again. At the moment, I was nothing more than a machine, motivated by impulses for revenge.

I hoped that Dawn would never see me like this, almost on a level with the animal, back at the stage where I had been a long time ago, wishing for a man's death, hoping that I would be the implement of his destruction. It certainly wasn't that part of me I would have liked her to see.

The Sergeant seated behind the high desk in the outer office of the local precinct had a face which looked as if it had been chipped from a solid block of granite. He eyed me suspiciously, listened while the taller of the two cops told the story, then pierced me with a narrowed stare.

'Johnny Merak, eh? I seem to have heard that name before.'

'A long time ago, Sergeant,' I said thinly. 'I'm a changed man now and I've friends back in L.A. to prove it.'

'Friends like Clancy Snow and Dutch McKnight?' he said with an odd edge to his voice.

'They're both finished,' I said. 'Clancy's dead and Dutch is serving a ninety-nine year sentence.'

'You don't say?'

'Sure I do.'

'Then who are your particular friends, Johnny. I've been out of touch for some time with happenings west.'

'Better get in touch with a guy named Grenville,' I told him and saw the look on his face change a little. 'He's the Federal Agent out there, or perhaps you haven't heard that either?'

'Sure. I've heard of him.' The edge to his voice had sharpened to a razor's edge. 'Don't try to be smart, Merak. Sure I'll check. Meanwhile, the Lieutenant wants a word with you. You seem to be a pretty important guy at the moment. Be careful you don't overstep yourself.'

'I'll be careful,' I said wearily. I was feeling beaten. My body ached and the strain of that near-drowning episode was beginning to tell on me. All I wanted to do was to find some nice bed, even if it was in a cell, and sleep for a week without wakening once. And the fact that I couldn't do it, made me want it more than ever.

'Through there,' said the Sergeant, jerking his thumb in the direction of a glass-panelled door.

I nodded and walked towards it. I seemed to have spent half of my life walking in and out of glass-panelled doors exactly like this one. I knocked, heard a voice shout, and walked inside.

The guy behind the desk looked up, waved me towards a chair. 'I'll be with you in a minute,' he said harshly.

Leaning back, I watched the other from beneath lowered lids. A thin, sandy-haired guy. He looked capable, a man who'd stand no nonsense from anybody. A straight cop, fair but sharp.

He riffled through the papers on the desk in front of him, then looked up. Offering me a cigarette, he waited until I had lit it, then said quietly, almost casually: 'You seem to be attracting trouble like a magnet wherever you go, Merak.'

'It follows me around, Lieutenant,' I agreed.

'Care to answer a few questions?'

'Sure, if they'll help. I'm at a loose end now. I've lost the guy I've been tailing.'

'I heard you had some trouble with a couple of hoodlums who wanted to toss you into the bay.'

I nodded. 'That's an unpleasant episode I'd like to forget as soon as I can, Lieutenant.'

'Sure, I'm not surprised. According to the reports I've received you're lucky to be still alive.'

I grinned. 'Everybody keeps telling me that. But I still failed in what I set out to do.'

'Save this guy Finton's life?' He raised a pair of quizzical brows. 'You did everything you could.'

He looked at me with more friendliness than I had expected after my meeting with the Sergeant outside.

'What's worrying me now, is where is Torlin at this moment? Where's he going to strike next? It seemed we had everything figured out once we knew who we were looking for, but it doesn't seem to have worked out that way at all. He's still out there somewhere, planning his next slaying. It could be anywhere, I suppose.'

'If it's any comfort to you, I've got a general alert out for him, and this man Harry Callen.'

'You might have difficulty with him. He's got connections back in Los Angeles. He's a big man there with a legitimate front so wide that you couldn't dent it with your accusations. And his lawyer is so smart he'd have him off the hook within hours unless you could really make it stick.'

The Lieutenant lit a cigarette and nodded. He blew a ring of blue smoke into the air and spoke through it. 'You seem to have that kind of evidence, Merak. Otherwise, they wouldn't think you were such a menace.'

'With what I know and what Harry Grenville has on them, it's enough to send both of them to the chair ten times over. And they know it. Callen must be scared for his own skin. He'd never have exposed his hand by coming here otherwise.'

'So, the rats are scuttling around, not knowing which way to turn,' smiled the other. His face was still hard. 'That's the way I like it. They're more apt to make mistakes that way.'

'These guys don't often make mistakes, Lieutenant,' I said soberly.

'Maybe not. But even so, the odds are shortening against them. The fact that Callen came here shows that he's no longer as sure of himself as he was.' The other sucked on his cigarette. 'I've sent a call through to Harry Grenville. He'll be here sometime tomorrow morning. Things are hotting up and the sooner we trap these two hoodlums, the better. Meantime, I reckon you'd better get some sleep. I've booked a room for you in one of the hotels. You're our star man at the moment, Merak, whether you like it or not.'

I got up, smiling, even though the effort hurt my face. 'I'll probably like it a lot better once I've had a good night's rest and Grenville is here,' I told him.

'I understand.' He nodded. I went out, past the Sergeant, who threw me a quick glance, opened his mouth as if to say something then seemed to think better of it.

One of the cops pointed out the way to the hotel nearby and I picked up the room which had been reserved by phone from the precinct. The manager gave me a funny look, seeing the bruises on my face, but passed no remarks. I had a steak, as tender as possible to ease the work on my aching jaws, went into the bar for a drink, then up to my room.

I took off my jacket and shirt. They were still damp and crackled a little with the dried salt in them. Pulling off my shoes, I lay back on the bed, took the old-fashioned Colt from my jacket and placed it carefully under the pillow. I wasn't expecting any trouble, not that night, but there was no sense in taking foolish chances.

I closed my eyes after switching off the light. Somewhere at the back of my consciousness, there was the sound of a car in the street below, but after that, nothing registered. It was morning when I opened my eyes again. A grey dawn was spreading slowly out of the east, touching the houses, lighting the objects in the room with a faint halo. I sat up quietly, fumbled for the packet of cigarettes in my pocket and lit one, leaning back again.

The ache was still there in my limbs whenever I moved, but not quite as bad or as persistent as on the previous night. My gun was still there where I had left it. I checked it again, then placed it on the table beside the bed. Outside, the city was beginning to stir. The streets were filling. The fog of the previous day had vanished sometime during the night and the air was clear, with a crisp, frosty sparkle that seemed to shine right through into the room.

By now, I thought, Harry Grenville would be almost at his destination. When he arrived, it might be possible to work out some plan to trap these men before they went any further with their diabolical plan. Four people dead and more to come unless we could stop them.

I swung my legs to the floor, stood up, and walked stiffly over to the window. There was a plane, just visible in the clear air to the south. Possibly the one on which Harry Grenville was coming to Chicago. I began to feel a little better inside. There was only one way to meet trouble, I thought savagely, and that was half-way. There was no sense in running away from it. Once you started that, you kept on running for the rest of your life. I had found that out in the early days when I had left all of that dirty work behind.

In spite of the feeling of warmth, I knew there was nothing ahead of me but trouble. It seemed a hell of a way to have to start a new day. I dressed slowly. Thrusting the gun into my pocket, I made my way downstairs for something to eat. Only now did I realise how hungry I really was, and when I had last eaten.

The food was good and I ate it slowly. My bruised jaw still felt tender as if I had been kicked in the face by a horse. I had just finished when the Police Lieutenant pushed his way through the swing doors and came over to my table.

I glanced up at him expectantly as he lowered himself into the chair opposite me.

'You had something to eat, Lieutenant?' I asked casually.

He nodded. 'I ate hours ago,' he said thinly. 'Small wonder that I get ulcers on this job. You're lucky, Merak, that you haven't got a desk job like mine.'

'Meaning you'd rather have bullets fired at you, than ulcers?' I grinned. 'You're likely to live longer, ulcers or not.'

'Mebbe you're right.' He stared morosely about the room. 'I've had a call from the airport. Your friend Grenville arrived on the morning flight. He'll be here in twenty minutes.'

'That's fine,' I said. I finished my coffee, lit a cigarette. 'I still wish I knew where Maxie Torlin was right now.'

'So do we all.'

'Hasn't that general alert you put out turned up anything?'

He shook his head, pursed his lips. 'Nothing so far. I've got road blocks out. Nobody can get out of town without me knowing. That's why I reckon he's still here somewhere waiting for the heat to die down a little before he makes another move.'

'There's one other possibility, of course,' I said.

'What's that?'

'He'd have had plenty of time to slip out before we found the body. Finton must have been dead for hours before I found him. Plenty of time for them to get out before you set up the road blocks.'

The Lieutenant's face fell wryly. 'Could be. But there's no reason why they should.'

'If you don't pick them up today, I reckon we'll have to consider that possibility.'

I got to my feet and followed him out of the hotel. His car was waiting beside the kerb and we drove to the precinct in silence.

Five minutes after we got there, Harry Grenville arrived. But I scarcely noticed him. Behind him, came Dawn, slim and graceful, her face uplifted towards mine, her eyes shining with something deep down within them that I would never understand. The aches and pains were forgotten for a little while, then I caught Grenville looking at me with an amused expression on his face.

'Let's get down to business, Johnny,' he said briskly. 'We've got plenty to do.'

We went through into the Lieutenant's office and this time, I noticed that the Sergeant behind the desk looked at me with a new kind of respect which had been missing the day before. He seemed like a guy to whom some tremendous revelation had just been made.

Briefly, the Lieutenant explained all of the machinery he had set in motion. Grenville nodded now and again, but said very little until the other had finished. Then he leaned forward heavily, resting his weight on his elbows. He seemed suddenly serious.

'I'm afraid that the birds may have flown by now, Lieutenant,' he said quietly.

The other looked surprised. With a slight shrug of his shoulders, he asked, 'What makes you think that?'

'We haven't been idle back in Los

Angeles. Since Johnny here, vanished so mysteriously twenty-four hours ago, we did some quick checking on anybody known to have been in with either Callen or Torlin, recently or in the old days. And we came up with several interesting facts. One of these was that Torlin intended to kill this man Finton. We were too late to stop that unfortunately. But we do know where he's going to get his next victim. It's a small town on the edge of the New Mexico desert.'

The Lieutenant lurched to his feet. 'Then if you know that, hadn't we better get started at once. I'll call in my men and alert every post along the way.'

'Somehow, I don't think that will be necessary. I've got men looking out for them. If our information is correct, Torlin doesn't intend to trust himself to public transport any further. He's going by car. It may take them the best part of two days to get there. We'll take the plane to the nearest point to this place and still beat them to it.'

It's a funny thing, but when you've been running around in circles like a cat with a tin tied to its tail, and you suddenly discover that you don't have to hurry any more, you can't believe it. I sat for several moments, trying to take in everything that Harry had said.

On the face of it, it didn't make sense, Torlin going by car, having to stop off at motels *en route*. But the more I thought about it, the more sense it began to make. He'd had a bad fright on that train from Los Angeles, when both of his body-guards had been knocked off, leaving him virtually defenceless. He wouldn't want anything like that to happen again. In a crowd, he would be unable to use his gun. In a car, with possibly another Cadillac filled with gunmen, he'd be both safe and secure.

'I've arranged for plane reservations on the next flight south,' said Grenville harshly. 'We ought to be there by tonight. Plenty of time to prepare a welcome for Callen and Torlin.'

'Who's going along?' I asked. 'I'd like to be in on the kill.'

'Of course, Johnny. You deserve that much.'

'And I'll come along if only for the ride,' said Dawn quickly, defiantly.

Her eyes swept over me, dark and enigmatic. 'There's no point in arguing, Johnny,' she said. 'I've made up my mind. I've seen what's likely to happen to you once I let you out of my sight. Besides,' she added sweetly, 'nothing can happen to me while I've two big men like you to look after me.'

'You don't know these men like we do, Dawn,' I said thinly. 'They're killers who'll stop at nothing, particularly if they're forced into a corner. If there's a showdown, you'll be in danger.'

She smiled and I knew that nothing I could say would make her change her mind. I looked at Harry Grenville, but he merely shrugged and the Lieutenant spread his hands on top of the desk in a universal gesture when I looked at him.

'It seems I'm outvoted,' I said at last. 'I only hope, for your sake, that nothing goes wrong with our plans. It's never safe to generalise where these two men are concerned.'

* ★ ★

We reached the airport half an hour before the flight was due to leave. There were few passengers for this particular plane and we took to the air on time. There had been little red tape. We were expected and the way was more or less cleared for us so that everything went smoothly.

Although I'd slept well the previous night, it hadn't been enough in my condition. I had that false feeling of well-being that comes from too little sleep. Settling myself down in my seat, I fastened my safety belt, felt the ground drop away beneath with the usual queasy sensation in the bottom of my stomach, and then we were gaining altitude and Chicago was a sprawling city once more, down below. I felt Dawn's hand slip into mine and somehow, even the feel of it made me relax. I wanted her near me, even though it could mean danger at the other end of the line; but that was still a couple of days away, I thought dreamily, let it all wait until then.

We had drinks on the plane and then settled down to the monotony of an air journey. The ground far below us changed almost imperceptibly beneath the drifting lacework of white cloud and fog. Once we got far enough south, November wouldn't mean a thing. It would be warm and sunny and we'd forget that there was ever such a thing as fog. Until then, we lazed in the inclined seats, thinking our own thoughts.

The eternal drone of the engines acted as a powerful soporific. In spite of myself, I soon dozed off, waking fitfully whenever we hit an air pocket, but slipping back into exhausted sleep almost before the fact had registered. When I finally woke, and stayed awake, it was to find that it was late afternoon, and we were less than fifty miles from our destination. The country far below was rugged and mountainous, filled with long, stretching fingers of shadow thrown by the lowering sun. The air was clear, a deep, almost ice-blue and there was a thin crescent of a moon, just visible, swinging close to the distant horizon. In front of me, Grenville stirred and pushed himself upright in his seat. The stewardess came by, threw me a swift glance, arching her brows. I nodded.

'Rye on the rocks,' I said softly. Beside me, Dawn was still asleep, her head on my shoulder, her perfume heady in my nostrils. Even asleep, she seemed to present some strange enigmatic quality which no other woman I had ever known had possessed.

The stewardess brought my drink and I sipped it slowly, appreciatively.

'Not long now, Johnny,' said Grenville softly. He scarcely turned his head. 'I've fixed up reservations for us at one of the hotels here. We'll go on by car tomorrow morning. We still ought to be in plenty of time to meet our friends.' The way he said it made me feel almost sorry for Callen and Torlin.

I finished my drink. We were losing altitude slowly. Down below, the country remained the same. Open and wide, completely different from the teeming streets of Los Angeles and Chicago.

It was all yellow and harsh and glaring — hot. There was the desert all right, stretching away to every horizon. It looked empty and barren. But at least, it was one guy's idea of an ideal hiding place when you were running from death. They must have had one hell of a fright, I figured, to make them all run like this, scattering like chaff on the wind over the entire country. But I knew, also, that Torlin would have a twisted, warped pleasure in finding them like this, in hunting them down one at a time, no matter how far they had gone.

I rubbed the sleep out of my eyes, placed the empty glass on the tray in front of me. Dawn stirred, opened her eyes, then sat up, instantly awake.

'Where are we?' she asked.

'Nearly there,' I said. 'Another thirty minutes, maybe and we ought to be touching down.'

'And this man Torlin?'

'He won't be here for another twenty-four hours if Harry's right with his information.'

'I'm right,' said the other grimly.

The plane came down almost half an hour later. The town below looked small from the air when you were used to the big, sprawling places like the cities of the north. God knew what the hotels were like in a place like this.

We walked through the terminal and out into the main street. I was pleasantly surprised to find that everything seemed ultra-modern. There was a car waiting outside the terminal and Grenville walked straight towards it. The man behind the wheel, slim and olive-skinned looked as if he had just slipped in over the border and that at any moment, the Immigration Authorities might pop up on his tail.

'We received your message, Señor Grenville,' he said with a Mexican accent. 'Everything has been arranged as you asked.'

'Good,' Grenville nodded and motioned us into the car. He slipped in beside the man at the wheel, turning to us as the car shot away from the sidewalk with a tremendous burst of speed which almost hurled me through the back.

'This is an old friend of mine, Captain Salvadores of the Mexican police,' he explained. 'Perhaps I ought to put you completely in the picture, Johnny.'

'I'd be glad if you would,' I said. 'At the moment, there seems to be quite a lot I'm missing. I'm groping around in the dark here. Why bring the Mexican authorities in on this deal?'

'It is quite simple, Senor Merak,' said the Captain without taking his eyes off the road ahead. 'Senor Grenville believes that if everything goes according to plan, these two criminals may try to make a break for it over the border. I am here to help in case of that eventuality.'

I nodded. It was something I hadn't appreciated. Grenville, it seemed, wasn't taking any chances. At that very moment, somewhere along the dusty highway leading down from the north, the black Cadillacs would be racing south, bearing the big men to this final showdown with the law. Once they were concerned, they'd try every trick in the book. This time, Grenville didn't intend that there should be any slip-ups.

The hotel, when we reached it, proved to be modern and up-to-date, the rooms clean and spacious, the food excellent.

The Captain left us, promising to pick us up early the following morning. By now, it was almost dark. There was little twilight here, even in November, but the air was cool and crystal clear, and oddly refreshing after blowing off the Gulf of Mexico.

We ate our evening meal in silence, then retired. There would be a lot to do in the morning and I had that strange, tense feeling of inexorable time urging me on to some future I could not even contemplate.

In my room, I undressed and lay down on the bed. The window was half open and through it I could hear the sound of cars on the highway nearby and occasional voices. Normal, everyday folk, I thought, who cared little for anybody and whose lives were their very own, with little actual fear in them. I wondered with a faint feeling of self-pity, when such a life might belong to Johnny Merak, when he wouldn't have to jump at the smallest shadow, or have to carry a loaded gun around with him every minute of every day, just because he never knew when a bullet with his name etched on its leaden guts might be heading in his direction.

Where in the past had everything gone wrong for me, I wondered dreamily. There had been a time when it must all have started, when the merry-go-round had begun to swing with Johnny Merak on board, and then, somehow, it had got out of control, going faster and faster so that I couldn't jump without killing myself and I was forced to hang on and let it go with me as it would.

Start in on something dirty and you soon find that the big men have got you taped. Very few ever make the same break that I had done. Most of them had landed in the slums of the big cities with their kidneys ruptured, living out the few remaining years of their shortened lives in a pain-filled delirium from which there could be no mistake. Oh yes, I thought bitterly, the Organisation paid off — and paid off good.

When I finally fell asleep, it was into an uneasy, dreamless doze from which I woke several times for brief periods, only to fall asleep again. In the morning, when I woke with the sun in my face, there was that undefinable, nameless chill lying over me which I had experienced several times in the past and which almost always seemed to presage disaster.

The others were ready, waiting as I walked down to breakfast. I seated myself at the table and ate slowly.

'Something wrong, Johnny?' asked Dawn, looking at me sideways out of the corner of her eyes.

'I've got a feeling that something is going to go wrong today,' I said slowly.

By the time the car came with the Mexican Captain seated behind the wheel, the feeling had crystallised into real fear in my mind, but I tried to hide it from the others. Grenville seemed to know what he was doing, and as I followed him out to the car, I could feel, once again, that edge of ruthless cruelty to him which seemed to characterise everything he did.

11

Sucker Bait

I was beginning to feel better and worse. Better because at last, I had the feeling that we were doing something constructive about Callen and Torlin; worse because I knew that once the showdown came, it wasn't going to be as easy as Harry Grenville seemed to think. These men weren't fools, whatever else they might do. They'd been in this dirty business long enough to know most of the angles and to smell a trap a mile away. Not only that, but we still had to find this next victim of Torlin's; Harry said that his name was Sheldon, Mike Sheldon. Like the others, he had vanished from his home in Los Angeles almost a year earlier and had only been traced to this lonely, out of the way spot on the very edge of the New Mexico desert, by sheer chance.

But it was the one break we needed if

we were to finish this case before any more innocent people got themselves killed. I only hoped Grenville knew what he was doing, because for the first time, I was completely lost, out of touch.

I stirred in the rear seat of the fast car driven expertly by the young Mexican Captain. Clearing my throat, I said quietly: 'Just how are you going to work this deal, Harry? Got any fancy ideas about these two characters?'

'Some.' The other nodded. 'Remember, Johnny, I've had some dealings with these men before. You and I have seen them from different points of view. That's why I reckon we're so useful together.'

Coming from a man like Grenville, that was high praise indeed, but I ignored it at the time. I had a vision of the sleek, black cars, streaking through the morning sunshine, over the lonely roads, bearing their load of men to keep this date with death. If anything should go wrong . . .

'What about this guy we're trying to save,' I went on, 'any idea how we're going to get him out of sight without Torlin knowing that we're around. He can smell these things before he even sees them.'

'I've thought a lot about that, too. There's only one way we can do it and that's one of the reasons I need your co-operation, Johnny.'

'You've had that all the way along the line,' I said. 'You don't need to ask.'

'I knew you'd say that,' replied the other warmly, 'but you've been through hell already on this case that I wasn't sure how you'd take my suggestion.'

'Go ahead,' I said tightly. My voice was brittle, like an iron bar. I wondered what was coming next, but I guessed from the other's manner that it wouldn't spell great happiness for Johnny Merak. It didn't.

'Here's the set-up as I see it, Johnny.' Grenville leaned over the back of his seat while the Captain concentrated on his driving. 'We'll find this guy before Torlin gets on the scene. I've had the local police watching the place where he's hiding out. Fortunately, there aren't many people around this place, something of a ghost town nowadays. It'll make things easier for us if they come in shooting.'

'Go on.'

'We'll spirit this guy away and leave a decoy in his place. That way, they won't suspect a thing until it's too late.'

'And this decoy, this sucker? He'll be a guy who's handy with a gun, just in case.'

'That's right, Johnny.' For a moment, his voice sounded far away and tired.

'He wouldn't be a guy called Merak, would he?' was my next question.

Our car was rolling away over the flat, level country, along the first-class road which seemed coldly out of place in this area, roaring away the sixty odd miles to this hide-out. I listened, but didn't say anything further. I must have known that it would have been like this, right from the very beginning.

'I'm afraid so, Johnny. Captain Salvadores here, offered to take this man's place, but I need somebody who knows the type of man we're dealing with. Everything now could depend upon split-second action. No chance of a mistake.'

'Kind of dangerous,' said Dawn in a tight little voice.

'As far as men like this are concerned, everything is dangerous,' pointed out Grenville.

We rounded a long, wide curve, the tyres humming on the road. Out here, there seemed to be nothing but miles of wide, open country which stretched away into blue-hazed mountains in the distance. At least, here, I thought, there wouldn't be many holes into which these rats could crawl and hide. Once they showed themselves, it would be for good.

For a while, after that, we travelled in silence. The miles passed beneath the wheels of the fast car, eaten up in a blur of speed. The meeting with these hoodlums seemed to be a kind of symbol as I sat in the car, racing towards it. It meant something if only the end of the crazy obstacle race I had been engaged in for over a week now. But I didn't kid myself either way. It was going to be tough. Harry Callen and his troopers backing up this crazy maniac with a flair for killing. Those years in prison must sure have warped Maxie Torlin, I thought wearily. What I couldn't figure was why he went after the innocent people who tried him after he'd been double-crossed. Why didn't he go for the guys who'd framed him and set him up on his trial?

There had to be some peculiar twist in Torlin's mentality which didn't make sense. I couldn't figure it at the moment. Maybe if I'd had the chance to know him better, to prove behind that brain of his, I might have known the answers. As it was, if everything went right, there'd probably never be a chance of finding out.

I thought about Dawn and wondered what she was thinking at that moment. Maybe she thought it was a damnfool thing to try to do, three men and a girl against Callen's troopers. On the face of it, we didn't seem to stand much of a chance.

Grenville seemed to be absorbed in some private problem of his own and said little as the minutes passed. We slid through a couple of shanty towns that looked oddly deserted in the hot sunshine. I had the impression of faces peering at us from behind the tattered curtains, curious eyes, watching and wondering. But most of the way, it was just desert and scrubland, dotted here and there with stunted bushes. A dried-up, barren country, that slumbered fitfully in the sunlight. This could be what hell looked like, I thought dismally, and hoped that it wasn't an omen.

Twelve-forty. We ran through another ghost town and the Captain slowed the car slightly as we navigated several sharp S-bends in the road.

Five minutes later, the radiophones in the car burbled.

'Captain Salvadores ... Captain Salvadores ... '

The other flipped the switch. 'Salvadores here,' he said crisply.

'Message for Mister Grenville. I believe he's with you.'

Grenville took the phone. 'Grenville.'

'Forbes here, sir. You were right all the way. They headed south from here less than a half hour ago. Two Cadillacs, each packed with men. Are you sure you don't want me to send more men out after you. This lot looked as if they meant business.'

'We'll make out O.K.,' said the other.

'All right, sir.' The voice on the radiophone sounded dubious, but was not inclined to argue. 'Like you ordered, we didn't set up any roadblocks, but let them through. They don't suspect anything, I'm certain of that.'

Grenville grinned. 'So long as they believe that they have only some scared guy to take care of, they won't be too cautious. We'll just have to hit them hard and fast once they show up.'

'What about this man, sir. You're not leaving him there as a sitting target.'

'Not at all. I've brought along my own clay pigeon.' He turned his head and looked meaningly at me as he spoke. Flipping off the phone, he handed it back to the Captain.

'Everything seems to be playing itself out as we planned,' he said easily. 'That call means that they're still over a hundred miles away. It will possibly be around nightfall before they get to their destination. We still have plenty of time to set everything up, provided, of course, that our boy plays ball.'

'How are you going to get to him?' I

asked. 'He'll be as suspicious as hell. Any strangers in this place and he's likely to start blasting. He'll shoot first and ask questions later. And in his position, I wouldn't blame him. I know I'd take off after the first guy who showed his face who looked even the slightest bit like a crook.'

'That's a chance we'll have to take. I've got a loudspeaker fitted to the car. We'll hail him once we get within distance. I'm banking on making him see reason.'

'It might not be so easy,' I said, trying to relax. The comforting feel of the gun which the Captain had so thoughtfully provided, felt cold and reassuring in my pocket. At least, we stood a chance. It was likely to be our last chance, but I tried not to think of that. More and more, I wished that Dawn had not been so stubborn as to insist on coming with us. I couldn't think clearly while she was tagging along. Bullets would start flying once those hoodlums hit this ghost town and from past experience on the streets of Los Angeles I knew that slugs were no respector of persons.

I lit a cigarette. My eyes felt like grit, smarting and tender. The glare from the desert on either side was beginning to make itself felt.

When we finally rolled into the tiny ghost town, it was almost three o'clock. It looked empty, quiet. Too quiet. We stopped the car at the end of the narrow, dusty street and got out slowly. For all we knew, there might be a rifle trained on us at that very moment, a finger itching on the trigger. I began to get that queasy feeling deep down inside my stomach again. This wasn't turning out the least that I had expected.

Grenville cupped his lips. 'Sheldon!' The slant-roofed buildings made a mockery of his voice as they threw back the echoes, chasing each other along the solitary street.

No answer. We hadn't really expected any, but it only served to make our task more difficult and dangerous. This guy was potentially a killer. A man crazed by fear, not knowing when death would strike. But he would have armed himself and he'd be watching. Possibly he had seen us drive up. In a place like this, the dust cloud kicked up by the car would have been spotted miles away on the horizon, and the sound of the powerful engine could have been heard half a mile away at least.

'Mike Sheldon.'

Silence after the echoes had flapped between the houses and died away.

'He could be hiding away anywhere in this dump,' I said loudly, casting about me for any place which immediately stood out. 'It'll take hours to find him.'

Without a word, Grenville walked back to the car, slipping in behind the wheel. A moment later, the loudspeaker came to life, his metallic-sounding voice vibrating through the ghost town.

'We're the police, Sheldon. We know that you're hiding from Max Torlin and that he's coming after you with a squad of hired killers. He won't hesitate to shoot you down like he did the others. We're here to protect you. That's why you've got to trust us.'

There was a click, then silence. I could almost hear the hands of my watch grinding their way around the circular face. For all the sound there was, the entire place might have been dead for the past fifty years with only the rats left behind.

Then, from somewhere further along the street, a thin, harsh voice shouting: 'Don't try to fool me like that, you lousy punks. I've got a rifle here trained on you and plenty of ammunition.'

'Don't be a goddamned fool, Sheldon,' yelled Grenville. He no longer needed to use the loudspeaker. 'Do we look like crooks? This is Captain Salvadores of the Mexican police.'

'That uniform doesn't fool me either, mister. You probably got it off some cop you've knocked off.'

'We're getting nowhere fast,' I said harshly. 'And the trouble is we can't rush him. That really would convince him that we're Torlin's men.'

Stalemate. What to do when you're doing your damndest to save a guy's life and he persists in believing that you're the very guys who're coming to knock him off?

I stepped out into the middle of the street where he could see me. 'Listen, Sheldon. I'm coming in to talk with you. Keep that rifle trained on me if you like, but watch your trigger finger. This may be the only chance you'll have of saving your life, so don't pass it up now.'

A pause, then the harsh voice again: 'All right, mister. Just move forward very slowly and don't make any sudden moves. If you think I'm going the same way as the others, you're mistaken.'

I walked slowly along the street. I could feel Dawn's eyes boring into my back and I wondered how well my hunch was going to pay off. A guy like this must be nearly at the end of his tether and a man in that position was potentially more dangerous, more likely to shoot to kill, than any hoodlum.

'All right, mister. That's far enough. Speak your piece and then get back to your friends before I start shooting.'

'You're on the wrong track this time,' I said quickly. I could just see him behind the shattered window of the house a few yards away. The sunlight glinted on the barrel of the rifle that was pointed at my chest. At least, he hadn't been kidding about that, I thought wrly.

The rifle never wavered by so much as an inch, but I knew that he was also watching the others out of the corner of his eye and I hoped that none of them would make any wrong move or there'd be a bullet in my chest.

'That guy back there is Harry Grenville,' I said slowly, forcing evenness into my tone. 'He's a Federal agent from Los Angeles. We know all about this man Torlin and his association with Harry Callen. They've tried to kill me three times already. Just because I know too much. I was a couple of hours too late to help Finton back there in Chicago, but I'm in time to help you, if you'll only give me the chance.'

'Keep talking,' said the other. 'And you'd better make it good.'

I breathed a little more easily. 'Torlin and Callen, with a bunch of their picked gunmen are on their way here by car. We've had their route checked all the way. We flew here from Chicago to beat them to the punch. What we want you to do is to get out of here. Captain Salvadores will see that you're out of danger and I'll take your place here. It's the only chance we have of trapping them all.

'We've only a few hours in which to get everything set up. Think it over if you like, but don't take too long or it may be too late to help you.'

'How do I know you're telling me the truth?'

'You don't. That's something you've got to say on trust. But do you think if we were hoodlums, we'd be parleying with you like this. Isn't it more likely that we'd be blasting that shack about your ears by now.'

There was another pause, longer this time. Then I saw a movement behind the window and a moment later, he stepped out into the red sunlight of the street, still gripping the rifle tightly in his right hand. He was a tall, wiry guy, about my own height with a lean, tanned face. His eyes held a haunted look and I doubted whether he had had a good night's sleep for several weeks. I took his arm and walked with him back to the car.

'Now you're showing some kind of sense, Mr. Sheldon,' said Grenville. 'Once we get you out of sight, we'll set up our little trap. Everything has to work perfectly, because the rats we're after are pretty big ones. And they're bringing a carload of thugs with them, just in case of trouble.'

'You think you can stop them — the three of you?' muttered the other, his eyes widening in surprise as he cast about him, hoping to see more police cars drawn up out of sight.

'We'll make it. If you care to take your chance with us, all right. But we aren't asking you to expose yourself to any danger. We're getting paid for this.'

'I'll do anything you ask me,' said the other quickly. He looked like a guy who had just let slip a tremendous load from his shoulders. The world seemed new and fresh to him once more.

'Good. Then let's get to work. We haven't any time to waste. I'll give them another couple of hours. First of all, we'll have to get the car out of sight, but somewhere where we can use it in a hurry. If they try to make a break, we may have to use it as a roadblock. Fortunately, the trail ends here. I doubt whether they could take a car beyond this place. The going is so rough they'd rip their tyres to threads before they'd got fifty yards.'

'That means we only have to block the trail into the place,' said Dawn.

'Right. So I figure that if we can park the car out of sight among those shacks there at the edge of the road, ready to run it out if necessary, we should be all right. It ought to be dark by the time they arrive and they won't be expecting trouble. It may make them just that little bit careless.'

Captain Salvadores drove the powerful car out of sight, then came back.

'All ready,' he said unnecessarily.

'Good,' Grenville nodded his head, turned to me. 'You know what to do, Johnny?'

'I reckon so. I'm to sit in that place back there, just showing myself and risk being shot at.'

'I wouldn't put it that way, but I

suppose it all boils down to that in the end. Don't take any unnecessary risks. We'll move in once the trap is set.'

'Don't delay too long before you come in,' I said pointedly. 'And be careful where you're putting those bullets. I'll probably be right in the middle of them.'

I made my way along to the shack just vacated by Sheldon. It smelled of dry wood and other indefinable odours which I couldn't place. Not a nice place in which to die, I thought wryly. I could see why the other had chosen it as his hiding place. It commanded an excellent view of the street in both directions, projecting as it did a little way in front of the others. But that single characteristic made it stand out from the other buildings and it might give these hoodlums an idea of where to come.

Settling myself down as comfortably as possible in front of the window, I steadied the rifle which the resourceful Captain Salvadores had provided against the broken sill of the window, checked the heavy pistol and placed it down carefully beside the other weapon.

Outside, there was silence. I could just make out the shadowy figures of Grenville and Salvadores at the far end of the street, but there was no sign of Dawn or Sheldon. I guessed they'd already be under cover. My watch said six-fifteen. I threw a swiftly apprehensive glance at the reddening sky. Another hour or so before it was really dark, I figured. By then, the hoodlums would probably be here, scouring the place for Mike Sheldon. I tried to put myself into Torlin's mind, to figure out how he would go about it.

There was no doubt that he would insist on killing his victim himself. That had been the one basic pattern behind all of the other slayings and I saw no reason why he should alter his tactics now. Besides, it seemed to be part of his make-up, his ego, to let his victims know who it was that pulled the trigger which blasted them into enternity.

Nothing to do now but wait. Time passed very slowly, squeezing itself by like something out of a tube. The desert, which lay on all sides of the shanty town, was quiet and unmoving, as it had been for centuries. Sound would travel far in that quietness, I thought, and I ought to be able to pick out the sound of a couple of high-powered Cadillacs nearly a mile away.

It wasn't likely that they would park their cars any great distance from the place and walk the rest of the way on foot. Or would they? It might be the kind of thing Torlin *would* do. As far as he was concerned, they were up against only one man; a badly frightened man, who might or might not be armed. Even if he were, a dozen men could take him easily and there would be no need for a quick get-away. Besides, if they stopped the cars somewhere out there along the desert road, they could come in silently and take their victim unawares, thereby minimising the danger from any weapon he might have. They were neither stupid enough, nor heroic enough, to want to get themselves killed if there was another alternative.

For what seemed the hundredth time, I checked with my watch. The sun had touched the horizon with a fiery glow, and was slipping down into darkness like an oversized penny dropping into a black box. The wind lost some of its warmth and blew coldly through the cracks in the splintered woodwork.

I shivered and it was not all due to the cold. There was a sound in the distance, a familiar sound, very faint at first, but unmistakable and coming nearer, getting louder. Maxie Torlin coming to keep an appointment with Mike Sheldon. I checked the rifle, slid the bolt back until there was a cartridge in the breech and slipped off the safety catch.

No sign of the others. They were crouched down out of sight somewhere, waiting tensely to spring the trap. I smiled bitterly, in the dimness. This was a new role for me in a way. Johnny Merak, fall-guy, clay-pigeon for a gang of hoodlums. Sucker bait!

The sound in the distance had stopped. The desert was quiet again. Nothing moved. I could hear my heart thumping like a steam hammer inside my chest, battering painfully against my bruised ribs. They'd be coming in for the kill now.

I doubted whether any would be left with the cars. There was nothing to fear, out here, miles from anywhere. Only one frightened guy in the middle of this wilderness, waiting for death.

I could visualise the glee on Torlin's face, the anticipation which would be building up to explosion point inside him. His mind was like a time bomb, set to go off at predetermined intervals.

Narrowing my eyes, I watched the road leading into the shanty town. I didn't think they'd bother with circling around the place and coming in from all sides. Twelve thugs who'd learned their lessons the hard way, against one guy. Those were the kind of odds these people liked and relished. Nothing could go wrong.

It was several minutes before I spotted them. They came walking forward in the deepening twilight, in a loose bunch, scorning any cover until they reached the end of the street. I could see the bulky figure of Maxie Torlin a little in front of the others, almost hurrying, as though there were some dreadful hunger inside him which had to be fed, something which drove him on, urging the others on too.

They stood quite still at the end of the street, peering forward into the darkness. I tensed myself, picked up the rifle and balanced it carefully on the ledge of the window, squinting along the sights. Torlin was right in them. Convulsively, my trigger finger tightened of its own accord.

The others came up too. They looked a tough, murderous bunch even though I could scarcely make out their faces. They held their hands in their pockets and I guessed their fingers were curled around the triggers of their guns.

'All right, Sheldon,' shouted the familiar voice. 'This is the pay-off. It's no use hiding from me any longer. I know you're here and you're as good as dead right now. Only I want you to know who it is who's going to kill you.'

12

The Pay Off

I gave no answer to Torlin's shouts. I wanted him closer than that before I revealed myself. At the moment, they were too far away for the trap to be sprung with any chance of success. Torlin paused, uncertain. He kept jerking his head from side to side, listening, wondering where the man he wanted to kill was hiding out. I could sense that the silence was beginning to get on his nerves. The other killings had been done in the city where there was plenty of blare and noise. Out here, it was different.

After a while, he walked forward again. This time, he had a gun in his right hand, the others walking on either side of him along the quiet street. I saw Harry Callen and felt a sudden thrill of satisfaction. We had the whole bunch of them here, right in our grasp, so long as nothing went wrong. I wondered how long Grenville intended to hold his fire. Possibly until I opened up. For the moment, I was the focal point of the whole drama.

Ten yards from the window, I saw Torlin pause. The gun in his hand wavered a little. He was no longer quite as sure of himself as when he had entered the place. There were too many shadows in which a man might hide and shoot him down. I could see that he was scared slightly. Too many places from where a bullet might come.

'Sheldon?'

I waited until his head was turned the other way, then said softly, my voice carrying into the darkness. 'That's far enough, Torlin. This is the end of the line for you.'

He whirled like a madman and his voice was almost a scream. 'Merak! This is some kind of trick. You can't be — '

'Can't be alive, Torlin? Want to take a bet?'

Two of the hoodlums jumped to one side, went down onto their faces and began firing blindly in my direction. I heard the slugs crunch into the dry wood of the windows and one hummed dangerously close to my head, smashing into the wall behind me.

I pressed the trigger of the rifle, saw Torlin stumble as the bullet took him. Then the night was made hideous with the sound of rifles and heavy automatics.

It didn't take the hoodlums long to draw a bead on my hiding place. They made no attempt to run for it, although a couple of them slipped away, crabwise, into the shadows on the far side of the street and flung themselves under cover. More muzzle flashes out of the darkness. More slugs tearing into the woodwork, burying themselves in the ledge in front of me.

One tall guy, trying to be a hero, pulled himself to his feet and tried to rush me. Dropping the rifle, its magazine empty, I snatched up the Luger and fired instinctively. The bullet took him in the left knee and he stumbled forward onto his face with a wild scream of agony, the gun in his hand discharging itself harmlessly into the street in front of him.

He tried to pull himself along on his hands and knees, dragging the shattered limb behind him. A bullet from further along the street pitched him forward onto his face in the dirt and he lay still. Another guy, running wildly back along the street, was met by a fusillade of fire and collapsed in a heap with a dozen slugs buried in his quivering flesh.

It was a sharp fight while it lasted which was perhaps ten, fifteen minutes. When it was over and there was no more firing from the huddled bodies in the street, I slipped a fresh clip into the Luger and walked out of the house. From further along the street, the others came out into the open, Grenville prodding the guy who had been killed when he had tried to run, with the toe of his shoe. When there was no response, he shrugged and caught up with the others.

'I guess that's it finished as far as these hoodlums are concerned,' he said dispassionately.

'Where's Maxie Torlin?' I asked thinly.

Grenville pointed. Maxie lay face-upwards in the dirt, his lips twisted back into a sneer of almost demonaical hatred, his teeth showing brightly in the dim shadow of his face. His hands were glenched tightly by his sides and the gun was still in his right fist so that we had to prise his fingers apart to loosen the grip. He had died like his victims, with several bullets in his chest, the front of his immaculate shirt stained with his blood.

'He's finished,' said Captain Salvadores tightly. 'He will kill no more.'

'At least that's something to be thankful for,' said Dawn. She shivered.

I walked around the dead men lying in the middle of the street, then crossed over to the other side and located two more, crouched down in death in the shadows. I checked their faces. Most of them were new to me and I figured that Torlin had hired them in Chicago. Not until I had rolled over the last one did I realise that something was wrong, terribly, dreadfully wrong.

The other hurried forward. 'What is it, Johnny?'

'Harry Callen. He isn't here. He must have got away during the firing.'

'Are you sure?' His voice was like an iron bar, tight and brittle.

'Positive.'

'Was he with them?' asked the Captain.

'He came along with Torlin. They were together until I opened fire. Then Torlin went down. I didn't see Callen after that.'

'If he's heading for their cars, we'll stand a good chance of cutting him off,' muttered Grenville. He started along the street. The others followed him. I started to, then hung back. There was another possibility, one which demanded more urgent attention. Callen must have reasoned by now that we had a car stashed away somewhere in the near vicinity. If he wanted to make his get away, it was more likely that his scheming brain had figured on using ours. Not only was it likely to be nearer than his own, but if he could get it, then it would mean we would have to tramp several hundred yards to theirs before we could take off after him.

The others were at the end of the street and cutting along the desert trail by the time I reached the end of the shanty town and cut into the narrow space between the two shacks where the car had been hidden.

At first, as I edged my way cautiously around the corner, I thought I must have been mistaken. There was nobody there and the car was standing where it had been left. I began to breathe a little more easily, then paused. Something had moved at the very edge of my vision.

I turned my head slightly, then saw him. It was Callen, all right. There was no mistaking that broad shape. He came out into the open and moved flat-footed towards the waiting car. He was too far away for me to risk a shot. Noiselessly, I padded forward. No doubt he had been waiting in the shadows until he was sure that everybody had cleared town, heading for the other cars.

Ten yards to go. He had reached the door and was reaching out for the handle when I called to him: 'Don't try anything stupid, Callen, because I've been waiting for this for a long time. The rest of your gang are finished. You're the last; and you don't have much longer to go.' I covered him with the Luger, ready for any trick.

He stood quite still, staring at me with hatred written in his face and glaring out of his eyes.

'Damn you to hell, Merak. I ought to have killed you myself when I had the chance in Los Angeles.'

'That was your first big mistake then,' I said smoothly. 'It seems guys like you will never learn. You had to be in on the big deal with Torlin, didn't you. That's what's been your mistake.'

'Then why don't you kill me and get it over with, Merak?' he snarled.

I guessed he was deliberately trying to rile me, to make me act foolishly. His cunning, scheming brain would be busy right that very moment, trying to find a way of saving his skin.

'Look, Merak, the others aren't here. They won't know any differently. Let me go, and I'll see to it that you get a good slice of some dough I've got stacked away in Los Angeles.'

'Yeah?' I looked at him as though he were a leper, something unclean. 'That's a good one. Think I'd fall for something like that. I've been around, Harry. I know most of your tricks. Once back in Los Angeles, it would be the big fix for me. A carload of your hoodlums on some quiet street corner. A tommy-gun and I'd wind up the same way as the others, on a mortuary slab with my chest full of little holes.'

'No, Johnny. I mean it. I can make you a rich guy, one of the richest in the State. All you have to do is let me get out of here, make show that you haven't found me. Go running after the others—'

'You evidently didn't hear me plainly the first time,' I said ominously. 'I've been fighting rotten guys like you for almost a year now, ever since I really felt clean. That's why I went after Torlin.'

'But he was the killer, Johnny. I was never in on that deal?' He sounded on the point of hysteria.

'Then what are you doing here right now?' I asked. 'You could have stayed away, attended to your own business, and you wouldn't be on the wrong end of a gun by now, would you?'

I thought he was on the point of

nervous collapse, but Harry Callen wasn't quite finished yet. Without warning, he swung the door of the car hard against me, slamming the edge of it against my wrist. In spite of the fact that I had been expecting something like that, the move took me off balance. The gun dropped from my fingers as the sharp edge of the lock scraped deeply through the flesh on the back of my wrist. Savagely, Callen leapt forward for the kill, stiffened fingers probing for my eyes.

I leaned back, instinctively, riding the blow, jerking up my left hand in front of my face. His fingers jabbed into my hair and I hit him hard in the pit of the stomach. He reeled back against the side of the car, slid along it, the door slamming shut under his weight.

No time to scrabble around in the darkness for the fallen gun. By the time I got my hands on it, he could knock me cold with a rabbit punch on the nape of the neck. I jumped across him as he fell back, dropping all of my weight onto his chest. The air gushed from his lungs and he uttered a shrill scream of pain. But he still wasn't finished. He was fighting for his life, and a guy in that position seems to have the strength of ten men. His fingers gripped my ankle, twisting with all of his remaining strength.

Madly, I clung onto the side of the car, stamping down with my other heel. He hung on like a wild animal, clawing and kicking desperately. His breath was whooping in his lungs and his face was a mass of blood and sweat and dirt. His eyes were staring wildly with fear showing through in their depths. I stamped again on his throat and this time he uttered a wild bleat of agony and released his hold.

I stepped clear. He lay doubled up on the ground, hands clasped around his bruised windpipe, trying desperately to suck air into his lungs. His chest was heaving madly, legs threshing feebly. No more trouble from him for a little while, I decided, and bent to retrieve the gun. I found it a few moments later, hefted it into my right hand and stood off a little way, covering him, still not trusting him, even though he seemed to have had all of the fight knocked out of him.

There was the sound of running footsteps in the distance and a few moments later, Grenville appeared on the scene. He stared down at the shaking form of Harry Callen, then nodded brusquely. 'I see you had the same idea as just struck me, Johnny,' he said thinly, 'only fortunately for us, you thought of it in time.'

'He's in a pretty bad way,' I said breathlessly, 'I'm afraid I had to hit him hard.'

'He'll live,' said the other callously. He bent to examine the other, then straightened. 'Captain Salvadores is checking that the other men are dead. I've put a call through for a wagon to come out here and pick up the bodies. It seems that we've wiped out most of them in one blow. This is a pretty good night's work, Johnny.'

We waited in the silence of the ghost town for an hour until a mortuary wagon and a couple of police cars arrived from one of the neighbouring towns to the south. I watched as two of the men carried the still figure of Maxie Torlin into the back of the wagon.

Poetic justice, I thought grimly. He had died because he had never believed in failure. He had imagined that the organisation was so vast and so powerful that nobody could stand against it, that the power of evil and terror was supreme. He couldn't believe that somewhere there were men who were good and honest and honourable who wanted nothing of his type of regime, but who would fight, would even lay down their lives if necessary, to stop evil from spreading and taking root.

I walked over to where Mike Sheldon was standing by the side of the street. He turned as I came up to him and gave a weak smile.

'I reckon you can relax now, Mike,' I said in a friendly tone. 'It's all over. Finished. At least, as far as you're concerned.'

'I still find it hard to believe,' he said hoarsely. 'I've been living with this nightmare for so long that I thought it could never end. I knew he'd be coming for me, like he did the others. That's why

I came out here. I figured I might be safe from him here, but he must have found me somehow.'

'Men like Maxie Torlin have eyes and ears all over the country,' I told him grimly. 'They can find you where even the police are stymied. We were lucky that we managed to get to you before he did and we only did that because Grenville picked up a couple of Callen's men and threatened to throw the book at them.'

'What do you think will happen to this guy, Callen?'

'He'll get what he deserves, I reckon. I can tell you you've got nothing to fear as far as he's concerned. We've enough evidence to pin at least a dozen murder raps on him; and I guess he can only fry once.'

The other relaxed. I guessed he had been wondering whether the nightmare might still continue with Callen.

'So it really is finished then?'

I nodded. 'It's a pity a lot of innocent men and women had to die just so that it could all end out here,' I said.

'Why did he do it? I mean, why come

gunning for us? We only did our duty.'

'I've been trying to figure that angle myself. There must have been something twisted up inside his mind while he was brooding in San Quentin. Funny things can happen to a guy in there and I guess you couldn't say that Torlin was normal even before he went into prison. Probably, he was highly-strung, tight, too full of his own ego. He's been used to giving the orders and knowing that they'd be carried out to the letter.

'So when he was framed and sent up for six years, something must have snapped inside. The borderline between sanity and insanity is very thin. Sometimes, it doesn't even exist at all. I think it was like that with Maxie Torlin.'

'I think I'm beginning to get it,' said the other as we walked slowly along the quiet street towards the waiting car. 'He forgot all about the guys who'd framed him, thinking only about those who'd found him guilty.'

I nodded; held the door of the car open for him to get inside, then climbed in after him. Grenville crushed into the front seat and Dawn slipped in beside me. Now that it was all over, I realised just how tired and beat I really was. My face felt as if it had been pummelled all day and there was a dull ache low down in the small of my back.

Captain Salvadores started the car with a crashing of gears which seemed to be a characteristic of his race whenever they came into contact with a delicate piece of machinery such as an automobile.

'After this, all I want is a thick, juicy steak, tender so that it won't hurt these bruises on my face, and a tall whiskey,' I said, leaning back. 'Then I reckon I'll sleep for a week without caring what day it is.'

'I'll personally see to it that the steak and whiskey are yours, Johnny,' said Grenville, looking back over his shoulder, 'As soon as we get back to civilisation.'

'I'll take you up on that.'

★   ★   ★

It was still dark by the time we reached the hotel, but there were lights still blazing and the bar was open. We went inside, picked ourselves a table and ordered drinks.

'I must look kind of bad for this place at the moment,' I said, fingering my face.

'You look great, Johnny.' Dawn glanced at me across the table and I began to feel better.

There were still plenty of people in the bar even though it was almost dawn. The night life in this place seemed to continue well into the day and for once, I was glad of it. After a couple of drinks I began to disregard the aches and bruises.

Grenville grinned. 'Once the news of Torlin's death gets into the national papers, I reckon there'll be quite a lot of people who'll sleep better at nights,' he said quietly. 'To my way of thinking, it's a pity he wasn't framed for murder five years ago. If they'd sent that guy to the chair, it would have saved a lot of trouble.'

'We've got the chance to do that with Callen,' I said. 'I only hope that he doesn't slip out of the net when some smart, fast-talking lawyer gets in on his defence.'

'With what we've got on him back in Los Angeles, he doesn't stand a chance,' said Grenville positively. 'He's for the chair and the place will be a little cleaner without him. He's a hoodlum of the worst type, hiding behind a front of solid respectability. It's a pity we can't get at a few more guys who're doing the same sort of thing.'

'Maybe we will, Harry,' I said thickly, nodding. The waiter placed a steak in front of me. 'There's time yet for some of them to make a mistake as Callen and Torlin did. I've an idea, too, that this little affair is going to start things popping in the Underworld. It won't end here, in the desert, you know. It'll have repercussions all along the line.'

'Maybe you're right, Johnny. At least, I hope so. You know these people a bit more than I do. You know how they think and operate.'

'When we get back, you'll take a nice long vacation,' said Dawn firmly. She eyed me meaningly across the table. 'I think you've earned it after tonight.'

I tried to grin, but had to give it up.

'Maybe you're right, Dawn.' I chewed thoughtfully and gingerly on the steak. I could see Harry nodding out of the corner of my eye.

'O.K. O.K. I'm outvoted again.' I finished the steak in silence, leaned back in my chair.

Outside, the darkness seemed to be less intense and through the wide, glass windows, I could just see the dawn brightening along the horizon, lighting up the world. The sun wasn't far away, just out of sight. Pretty soon, it would be a new day.

I glanced at Sheldon. A new day for him, I thought, when he would no longer have to live with the nightmare of fear and terror, no longer jumping at every sound and shadow.

The sun came up like a penny out of a box. The lights in the crystal chandaliers dimmed, then went out altogether. The room was suddenly filled with the first red glow of sunlight.